The Case of the Misplaced Models

by

Tessa Barding

Improbable
PRESS

A SHERLOCKIAN ROMANCE

First published by Improbable Press in 2019

Improbable Press is an imprint of:
Clan Destine Press
www.clandestinepress.com.au
PO Box 121, Bittern
    Victoria 3918 Australia

National Library of Australia Cataloguing-In-Publication data:
    Barding, Tessa
    The Case of the Misplaced Models

ISBN: 978-0-648 5236-4-2 (pb)

ISBN: 978-0-648 5236-5-9 (eb)

Cover © Willsin Rowe
Design & Typesetting: Clan Destine Press
www.clandestinepress.net

Improbable Press
www.improbablepress.co.uk

For Susanne

CHAPTER ONE

THERE WAS LIGHT SEEPING UNDER THE DOOR GAP OF MY SMALL OPERATING room. Nothing was supposed to seep out of my operating room, not at 6.45 in the morning and definitely not without me inside.

I yanked the door open.

The room was dark except for the light above the operating table on which a young man sat, right leg stretched out before him, left one dangling from the table. He had taken off his trousers that lay, neatly folded, on the small chair next to the basin. A pair of well-worn Dr. Martens boots lay underneath it. He was looking at an ugly gash on his thigh with a frown, fingers tapping against the surgical stapler sitting next to him.

'May I ask what you intend to do with that thing?'

He raised his head by a mere fraction but didn't bother turning around. 'This needs to be taken care of.' He gestured towards his wound.

'It certainly does. Why aren't you at a proper A&E department?'

'Because the next A&E department is inconveniently located.'

'And this place isn't?'

'Precisely.'

'Breaking into a practice isn't an inconvenience?'

'Your security system is easy to bypass, and the door itself requires only the most basic of lock picking skills. It's more like opening a closed door.' He twisted his upper body around to look at me. 'Dr Watson, I presume?'

'Says so on my name badge, doesn't it. Now, let me have a look at that.'

I walked across the room and stood at the other side of the table, facing the patient. Seen from up close and in the merciless white light from above he turned out to be older than I had first thought him to be, maybe in his early thirties. He seemed in good physical shape. His outstretched leg showed the lean musculature of a long distance runner, there were no signs of malnourishment or neglect and at first glance no signs of drug abuse either. His speech was neither slurred nor did he speak with exaggerated enunciation, and, when I looked at his face, I found his eyes to be clear and focussed with a normal pupil reflex.

'Aren't you going to call the police?'

'Have you stolen anything? Helped yourself to a dose of narcotics?'

'No.'

'Have you destroyed anything on your way in? Damaged the door? The security system? Other than bypassing it, I mean.'

'No.'

'So the way I see it, you're just another patient arriving a tad early.'

He shot me a surprised look.

'Are you always that easy?'

'Easy?'

'About having your practice broken into?'

Of course I wasn't. Quite the contrary. I had told Robbie again and again it was about time we had the old security system replaced and that the lock on the main door was a joke. Our team had doubled in size, with Tim and Sheila having joined the year before, and we now had four fully stocked treatment rooms plus my operating room. It was only a matter of time before somebody other than this guy broke in, and not just to staple his own leg together.

Fact was, I was angry at myself for having forgotten my gym shoes at home – thus missing my morning workout; my landlord had given me notice because his daughter needed the flat; and this guy here was cute. Not twinky-innocent cute, but tall-lanky cute with sharp features and a pronounced chin. I liked tall and lanky.

'Well, didn't you just tell me your entering didn't qualify as breaking in?' I bent over his leg to take a closer look at the wound. It was a long, shallow cut that didn't look as if it had been caused by a knife. More of a tear, really. 'May I ask where you got that? And please don't tell me you cut yourself shaving.'

'I got stuck.'

'Uh-huh.' I looked up. 'Will you need a tetanus shot?'

'No, I'm all good.'

'Good. Let's get started then.' I held out my hand. 'Stapler, please.'

I put the stapler where it belonged and walked up to the cupboard to take out what instruments I would need and prepared a tray, slipped into a disposable surgery coat, donned mask and hat, and started scrubbing my hands and forearms.

Behind me, I heard my patient shift and grunt. When I turned around, I found him stretched out on his back, eyeing me suspiciously.

'You're not going to perform open-heart surgery, are you?'

'What?'

He made a vague gesture. 'Mask, coat and all.'

'Well, I don't intend to sneeze on you but it is a rather long wound. I'll have to clean it and then stitch you up. Better safe than sorry.' With one foot I pulled up my stool and sat down. 'Careful now,' I warned when I had adjusted the height of the table, 'this will hurt.'

He nodded his assent and I rinsed the wound carefully before cleaning it. Wherever he had got stuck, it had better been worth it, for the souvenir would remain with him for the rest of his life. Even cleaned up the injury looked ugly, and it would require more than the eight stitches I had thought it would take. With the exception of one single hiss at the very beginning of the treatment, not a sound came from him and I looked up to see if he had lost consciousness – happens more often than you'd believe, and it's usually not the members of the so-called weaker sex who faint – but his eyes were fixed on me.

'No anaesthetic,' he said when I reached for the syringe.

'You sure? That'll be some eleven or twelve stitches. You certain you want to do this to yourself?'

'It'll be fine. I'll live.'

I looked at him with raised eyebrows, but when he nodded again and closed his eyes, I shrugged and got to work. He lay perfectly still, fingers interlaced above his diaphragm, inhaling through his nose, exhaling through his mouth. Impressive.

'Done,' I finally said, satisfied with my work. He would keep a scar, obviously, but if it ended up an ugly scar, my stitches couldn't be blamed.

He sat up and inspected his thigh.

'Well done,' he approved. 'Looks better than anything I could have done with the stapler.'

'Thank you. All these years of training weren't for nothing then.'

He gave me a weak smile and moved as if to swing his legs over the edge of the table.

'Wait,' I said. 'This needs to be bandaged. You're not leaving like this.'

He huffed but stayed where he was while I removed gloves, mask, and hat and binned them, along with the coat.

'Do I need to tell you about aftercare?' I asked after I had bandaged his leg.

He shook his head.

'Want me to prescribe you some painkillers?'

Another resolute shake of the head, but when he got off the operating table to reach for his trousers, he had to lean against the sideboard for balance.

I rushed to steady him. The last thing I needed was an unnamed burglar fainting in my operating room.

'Are you certain you want nothing prescribed?'

'Painkillers,' he informed me, 'are deceivers. They cloud your mind and make you believe everything's just fine when in truth, it is not. And this will lead to a very wrong assessment of your current capabilities. I prefer to stay sharp and not let drugs lull me into false security.'

I shrugged. 'Your choice, your pain.'

He scowled at me, all but shook my hand off his arm and snatched his trousers off the chair to pull them on again. For a fleeting moment I considered helping him with his boots but decided against it. Let the stubborn git look after himself. I cleaned up my work area, rinsed the instruments I had used and put them into the steriliser. When I was done I turned around, half expecting the room to be empty but he was still there, leaning against the door.

'What, you still here?'

'Did you expect me to sneak off?'

'Given the fact that you sneaked in, well, the idea came to mind.'

'You wound me, Dr Watson.' He dug in his pocket and pulled out a few banknotes. 'What do you normally charge for the repair work you've just done?'

'Repair work?' I straightened and frowned at him. 'That, my dear boy, was a tad more than mere repair work. Must I remind you that you were about to use the stapler? Imagine what that would have looked like. Apart from the bloodbath, that is.'

'Well, treatment then. What do you normally charge for treatment such as this?'

'Normally my patients make an appointment and everything goes its normal and proper NHS way. But I don't assume you're inclined to provide me with your personal details.'

'You assume correctly. But you are right, I would have made a mess of my leg and it would not be right to run off without payment. So,' he flicked through his bills, 'how much?'

I pursed my lips. 'You know what,' I said slowly, knowing I would question my sanity later for what I was about to say. 'Consider it my Good Samaritan deed for this week and promise me you'll come back if anything is amiss.

'Here's my card.' I reached for the small tray that sat next to the computer, fished for one of my cards and scribbled my mobile number on the back. 'If you experience unusual pain, if anything feels wrong–'

'I promise to be a good boy and give you a ring,' he finished the sentence for me and took my card, cast a fleeting glance over it and put it into his pocket, along with the banknotes. Giving me a mock salute, he turned to go. 'I'll let myself out. You'll have your day to prepare, Doctor, and I've taken up quite enough of your time.'

'Oh no. You will not deprive me of the pleasure of seeing you out myself. Besides, we're about to open in,' I checked my watch, '20 minutes. Chances are good our receptionist will show up any minute.'

As if on cue, somebody knocked on the door.

'Come,' I called, and Jen's round face appeared in the door.

'Oh,' she said when she saw I wasn't alone. 'If I had known you had a patient scheduled in the middle of the night, I would gladly have got up an hour earlier.'

I groaned inwardly. Such a ray of sunshine, our Jen.

'It was an emergency,' my patient said, flashing her a boyish grin. 'I had an accident and your surgery was the closest I could find. I was grateful Dr Watson agreed to take a look and patch me up.'

'Well, lucky for you the good doctor has chosen to make one of his rare early appearances.' She shot me a venomous look. Must have detected my bike then. Maybe I shouldn't have brought it inside but it had been pouring when I had arrived here. 'Come along with me now, laddie, so we can get the paperwork sorted.'

Laddie? I was never sure whether it was a good or a bad sign when she got Scottish.

'There is no paperwork to sort out,' he said and adopted the look of a puppy well aware it had done something wrong. 'I'm a private patient, you see, and Dr Watson and I have agreed I would settle the account when I come for the check-up.'

Had we? I raised an eyebrow but the puppy look seemed to have the desired effect. Jen's features softened.

'A private patient then. Very well, Mr, uh–'

'Holmes,' he said with another charming smile. 'The name's Sherlock Holmes.'

I all but snorted. Sherlock Holmes? Well, it was certainly original, I'd have to give him that. I had treated a lot of 'John Smiths' back in the day.

Jen didn't seem to find anything funny about his name.

'Fine then, Mr Holmes. If you have an agreement with Dr Watson, I'm sure all is in order.'

'It is, Jen,' I hastened to assure her. 'I'll write up a report, no worries.'

'Holmes' flashed Jen another smile and, after wishing her a pleasant day, limped towards the main door. I followed him with my eyes until the door closed behind him and turned to find Jen giving me a hard stare.

'What?'

'Pretty, huh?'

'What is?'

'He is.'

'Yes.' I saw no reason to deny it. The team knew I was gay. It wasn't something I shouted from the rooftops, but I didn't lie about it, either.

'Sure you didn't show up early because of him?'

'Jen, please. I was here early because I wanted to go through the revised budget when I heard him at the main door.' No need to tell her about the break-in. 'Couldn't very well send him away, so I decided to stitch him up.'

She didn't look convinced, but I wasn't going to explain myself to our ill-tempered receptionist.

'And now if you'll excuse me, dearest, I will take a look at said budget. My first patient isn't due before 8.30, right?'

'Do you seriously expect me to memorise all of your appointments, Dr Watson?'

'No, of course not.' I looked over my shoulder to check if I had put everything where it belonged, and when I was convinced that, yes, the operating room was neat enough for the three small operations I had scheduled for today, I made for my office.

Chapter Two

The day turned out quite differently from what we had planned. Tim called in around nine, saying his youngest had to be rushed to the hospital, and he wasn't sure when or if he'd come in at all that day. His patients were divided between Sheila, Robbie, and me and by the time I realised I hadn't eaten since, well, since very early that morning, it was already four o'clock.

When Jen confirmed I had 30 minutes to myself, I went to get my jacket and changed into my outdoor trainers, left through the backdoor and headed straight to my favourite sandwich place that, luckily, wasn't too crowded this time of the day.

I treated myself to an overpriced but excellent sandwich and a latte, large, extra shot, checked the time and sat down on a bench in the small park across the street. I pulled out my mobile. Three messages: two from my landlord; one from Tony Stamford.

Humphreys' messages concerned the notice he had given me. He wanted me to move out as quickly as possible, and would I ring back at my earliest convenience? Right. Was I supposed to check into a hotel until I'd find a new flat or what?

Tony merely asked whether we were still on for the pub tonight, and, if yes, could we meet at 7.30 instead of 6.30. I texted back that yes, that was fine by me. And if he happened to know someone in need of a flatmate because it seemed I'd be without a home soon.

My phone rang almost immediately.

'You serious about that?'

'Hey Stamfs, unfortunately yeah, I am.'

'You know what? You're the second person to ask me that today.'

'What?'

'About finding a flatmate.'

'Yeah?'

'Yeah. A friend of mine asked me the same thing earlier this morning. He's got his eyes on a nice flat on Baker Street but doesn't think he can afford the rent by himself.'

'Really?' I asked, interested. Baker Street wasn't quite the location I'd have chosen for myself but hey, if the flat was decent and the bloke all right, why not.

'What's he like, your friend?'

'Weeell–' Tony hesitated, then continued, 'He's a bit special. A bit eccentric, perhaps. Nothing to worry about,' he added hastily. 'He's a freelancer, I think, doesn't keep regular work hours and isn't much of a people person. A bit of a loner, if you will. He's about your age, well, a couple of years younger, actually, but not much. In fact, I'm meeting him tonight. Want to come and see for yourself?'

'Sure, yeah. Where are you meeting, and when?'

'At 6.30. I got the address written down somewhere, gimme a sec.' I heard him rummage around in the background. 'Can't find it right now. I'll text it to you later, yeah?'

'Okay. Thanks, mate.'

I rang off. That didn't sound too bad. 'Freelancer' could mean anything, and, as for 'eccentric', well, that depended on the level of eccentricity. Then I rang Humphreys and left a message, asking him to call me back to discuss what exactly he had in mind. I'd moved into that sorry excuse of a flat well over three years ago, right after I'd signed up with our surgery, and I wouldn't be sent packing just like that.

I checked my watch and, seeing my next appointment was coming up, binned the sandwich wrapping and got up, finishing my latte on the way back.

A sprained ankle, a tonsillitis, yet another revised budget report, and a text with an address later and I was on my way to 221B Baker Street.

Tony met me outside the house, as agreed.

'He's upstairs already,' he said when I'd chained my bike to the fence. 'What's that about you needing to find a new place anyway?'

'Oh, Humphreys decided his daughter needed my flat, pronto.'

'Can he kick you out just like that?'

'Unfortunately he can. I was stupid enough to sign a periodic tenancy contract.'

'Bugger.' He made a sympathetic sound. 'Well, maybe you'll like this flat then. It does seem nice, I had a chance to look at it before you got here. Shall we?'

I nodded and followed him up a short flight of stairs. He rang the doorbell and the door was opened almost immediately. A slim, elegant woman who looked to be in her mid-40s stood before us, visibly annoyed.

'Dr Stamford,' she said, with barely suppressed rage, 'I know our mothers are good friends and I know I agreed to see your friend first, had I but known–' she interrupted herself and only now seemed to realise that Tony wasn't alone.

'Mrs Hudson,' he said with his easy smile, 'allow me to introduce Dr John Watson, another friend of mine. We went to university together and he has served in the Army until about four years ago. He's now working in a GP practice over in Southwark.'

Mrs Hudson's face lost some of its enraged expression and she held out her hand.

'Pleased to meet you, Dr Watson.'

'Likewise, Mrs Hudson.' She had a firm handshake and her eyes held mine in a direct gaze. 'I understand a flat-share would be agreeable to you?'

'That would depend on the tenants,' she said and gestured for us to follow her inside. 'The flat we're talking about is upstairs.'

I eyed the narrow staircase. Tony noticed and asked, 'Will you be all right with that?'

'Of course I will be,' I replied. 'It's an artificial knee, Tony, not a prosthetic limb.'

It had actually been a shattered shinbone along with a shattered knee that had ended my military career, and while my new knee cooperated nicely, the lower leg still caused problems every now and then, especially in cold and wet weather. The handrail looked sturdy enough, however, and I should be all right even on a bad leg day.

'War injury,' I told Mrs Hudson who gave me a questioning look. 'Stairs have lost some of their appeal since then, but this looks manageable.'

She nodded and we followed her upstairs. The door was open, and a short and narrow hallway led into the living room where a tall man stood with his back to the door, looking out of the window. He was wearing a black leather jacket, black trousers and a pair of well-worn Dr. Martens. When he heard us coming, he turned around.

'Dr Watson,' he said with a crooked grin. 'We meet again.'

Chapter Three

I noticed I was gaping and closed my mouth.

'I had no idea you two know each other,' Tony said. 'Well, that will make things a lot easier, won't it?'

'We don't really know each other,' I replied. 'He showed up this morning at the practice, I patched him up and that's about it.'

'Oh, Sherlock, what have you done now?' Tony looked dismayed. 'You didn't tell me you had an accident. What happened?'

So Sherlock Holmes was his real name after all. I could have sworn he'd made it up.

'Nothing to worry about. All good. Dr Watson has done a very fine job indeed.'

He grinned at me. 'I believe proper introductions are in order now that we're considering a flat-share. I'm Sherlock Holmes, and I am pleased to make your acquaintance, Dr Watson.'

He held out his hand like a good little boy and I took it, half expecting him to bow, given that he seemed on his best behaviour.

'John Watson.'

He didn't bow, merely nodded his head, and his eyes scanned me from head to toe, making me feel like an insect under a microscope. Apparently I wasn't found lacking because he nodded again and let go of my hand.

'Shall we?'

'Shall we what?' I asked.

'Look at the flat?'

'Oh. Yes. Of course.' I turned around to where Mrs Hudson was standing, the look of disapproval still lingering on her face. 'Do you have time to give us a tour or should we look around ourselves?'

She checked her wristwatch. 'I guess a quick tour would be in order.'

Sherlock flashed her the same winning smile he had bestowed on Jen this morning. 'Thank you very much. I promise we will not delay you, and you will make your dinner appointment in time.'

'My...how did you know I had a dinner appointment?' She narrowed her eyes.

'Your make-up is immaculate and hasn't settled into creases yet which tells me you've either just applied it or thoroughly touched it up. Your shoes and nylons are dry and clean despite the fact that it's rained all afternoon. Just look at Dr Watson's trouser legs, for example.'

I looked down. There were splashes all over my trousers which was hardly surprising. I had come here by bike, after all.

Sherlock rattled off a few more things about jewellery, how the faint rustle of her nylons indicated she had just put them on, her choice of perfume, and the way she had done up her hair until Mrs Hudson raised her hands in protest.

'Thank you, that's quite enough, Mr Holmes. With your permission, I should like to show you the flat now.'

And it was a nice flat, too. The living room was partially furnished with two comfortable looking armchairs and a set of bookshelves. It had a fireplace, and images of sitting by a cosy fire, reading or relaxing, danced through my mind. I liked the idea.

A nice kitchen with enough room to put a table into, and the bathroom had a claw foot bathtub with a shower head. I preferred taking a shower over bubble baths anytime but the claw foot model did have a certain charm. The rather improvised shower head construction needed to go, though. I would change that to something sturdier and add a shower curtain, too.

Two bedrooms, one across from the living room with a built-in wardrobe, and the second one could be reached via some chicken ladder-like construction that I didn't like at all.

'I'll take the upstairs bedroom,' Sherlock said when we reached the living room again. 'It'll be no good for your knee, and I'll have access to the roof.'

I shot a glance at Mrs Hudson, hoping she had missed the last remark. She was busy exchanging pleasantries with Tony and, from what I overheard, he was doing his best to smooth her still-ruffled feathers. Bless him and his soft heart. He couldn't bear people to be unhappy around him.

'How do you know about my knee?' I asked Sherlock, wondering what had given me away.

'You favoured your left leg when you climbed down,' he said and added, as if on second thought, 'And I caught your remark about an old war injury before you came upstairs.'

'I see. Thank you. But the room is smaller than the other one.'

Sherlock shrugged. 'It's big enough for a bed, a lamp and a small wardrobe. Mind letting me use a third of yours? Wardrobe, I mean?'

'Sure,' I said. 'I don't have an awful lot of clothes.'

Mrs Hudson turned around. 'Well? What do you think?'

'I like it,' I said. 'It's a very nice flat. Would you consider renting it to the two of us?'

She didn't reply right away, pursed her lips and gave Sherlock a long, thoughtful stare. After a moment, she sighed. 'Very well. Here's what I will need of you.'

She produced two sheets of paper from the slim briefcase she had tucked under her arm and handed them to us. I glanced over mine. Proof of identity, employment status, credit records, references…the usual. Sherlock folded his copy and put it into his inside pocket without looking at it.

'My brother will be in touch,' he said, as if that explained all. 'I play the violin. Is that going to be a problem?'

'No,' Mrs Hudson replied. 'This is an old house with thick walls. Any pets?'

I cleared my throat. 'I have two guinea pigs.'

Two sets of eyes bore into me. Tony hastily covered his mouth to hide his grin.

'Guinea pigs?' Mrs Hudson sounded incredulous. 'Well, I suppose they're in a cage, yes?'

'They are,' I assured her. I usually let them run free in my apartment when I was at home but didn't think she needed to know that. They weren't vermin, didn't carry diseases and didn't particularly care about cables and wallpaper. 'My nieces left them in my care when they moved to New Zealand.'

Her face softened a little. 'I understand. That was very nice of you. They shouldn't cause any problems.'

'None at all,' I said in a firm voice.

We said our goodbyes and promised Mrs Hudson we would provide the requested documents by the end of the week, and she in return promised to let us have her decision shortly. Sherlock took his leave and Tony and I made for the pub.

'So,' Tony said after a while. 'Do you think you'll get along with him?'

'I can't see why not. He seems an all right bloke. But I get what you meant about him being eccentric. That thing of his, you know, throwing facts about yourself into your face, that may take a while getting used to, but I think he's a good one.'

And sexy as hell, I thought. God, I liked how he moved, and he sure knew how to wear his trousers. He had the kind of lean, angular build that looked bony at first glance, but as I'd seen him half out of his clothes this morning I knew better.

A thought occurred to me. 'I didn't tell him I'm gay.'

Tony shrugged a shoulder. 'Sherlock doesn't label,' he said. 'To be honest, I don't even know which team he's on. Why, do you fancy him?'

'He's not bad,' I said evasively. 'But that's not why I said it. Should I mention it when we sign the lease? If we get the flat, that is.'

'I don't think he cares. If he doesn't already know.'

'How so?'

'That thing of his, as you called it? You haven't seen half of it. He can tell by the way your shoes are tied what song you heard last and whether you prefer cornflakes or toast for breakfast.'

'You have got to be kidding me.'

'Oh no, I'm not,' Tony replied earnestly. 'He's probably deduced you're gay the second he laid his eyes on you, quite possibly this morning at the practice, and I wouldn't bet against him already knowing about your guinea pigs when you walked into the room.'

I snorted but Tony nodded solemnly. 'You'll see.'

'Ah well,' I said. 'It can't be that bad. What will you have, Stamfs? I'm buying the first round.'

Two weeks later we signed the lease, and my life with Sherlock Holmes began.

CHAPTER FOUR

IT STARTED OUT NICE ENOUGH. THE MORNING I MOVED INTO 221B BAKER Street was a typical English spring day, grey and overcast, but dry, thankfully.

It didn't take long to haul my belongings upstairs and put bed, sofa, and shelves back together, and when my helpers took their leave, I promised the next pub night would entirely be on me, which earned me cheers and warnings to start saving.

I knew they'd hold me to my promise, but that was all right. Not one of them had developed sudden back problems, nobody's family had had to face an oncoming plague, nobody's cousin thrice removed had died – they'd promised to help and had all shown up on time. Well, all but Karim who was travelling, as usual, but I didn't hold that against him as his job often required him to travel at short notice.

Sherlock had mentioned he was going to move in the day before me and, when we arrived, there was indeed some stuff in the living room, but he wasn't around and remained absent long after the lads had left.

I'd have liked to talk things through with him – what was to go where, who'd use which space in the fridge, in the freezer, in the bathroom cabinet; would we mix our cutlery and crockery or would this be a 'my space – your space' kind of arrangement?

Well, I'd start unpacking, and if there were things he felt needed further discussing, then discuss them we would.

About half of my wardrobe was taken up already and I raised my eyebrows as I inspected the extent of the invasion. *'Borrow a third'*, or so Sherlock had said. Well, well.

I glanced over the row of suits and jackets that lined the rail – classic colours, most of them, dark blues, greys, even a pinstripe. From what I'd seen of Sherlock so far, I would not have taken him for a suit person. But then, we'd only met on three occasions, and I had no idea what he did for a living. He could very well be a freelance consultant working for the banks and law firms – the business district crawled with them, and they came in all shapes and colours.

My clothes, shoes, books, CDs and DVDs were out of their bags and boxes and sorted into shelves and wardrobe in no time. I'd been in the military for too long and had moved too often to hoard a lot of things and hoped this would change. Not the hoarding part but the moving around bit. I was tired of packing and unpacking, and I was quite ready to settle down for a while, and this flat looked nice enough to make it my home for the next couple of years.

I really hoped Sherlock and I would get along because I wasn't too keen on living by myself. It wasn't as if I didn't know what to do with myself, but I liked having company, I liked shared meals, I liked a chat over breakfast.

Loud squeaking brought me out of my musings and back into reality. The guinea pigs. I had forgotten all about them for a moment. They were still sitting in their transport box and were probably fed up and hungry so I quickly got their cage ready.

'Welcome home, boys,' I said, taking them out of their box. 'You'll bunk with me until I've decided on your spot.'

No reply. They vanished into in their little house, muttering to themselves, probably pouting and cursing me out.

The kitchen was next. The table was occupied by a microscope, something that looked like a Bunsen burner and – were these preparation slides and dishes? Was Sherlock a hobby chemist? If that was the case, we would definitely have to sit down and talk because experiments and food? Not a good combination if you ask me.

The cupboards on the wall were empty when I opened them for inspection, as was all other storage space. A few plastic boxes sat in the fridge, but the freezer was empty. Fine. I'd just spread out as I saw fit and start cleaning.

'JOHN, WHY ON EARTH are you scrubbing the bathroom?'

I started. Sherlock was standing in the bathroom door with an expression on his face that was half puzzled, half accusing.

'Because it's too dirty for me to want to use it?' I offered and wiped my wet hands on the towel. 'Hello, Sherlock.'

'You really don't need to do that. I've arranged for a cleaning squad to swing by tomorrow.'

'A cleaning squad?'

'Well, yes.' He gestured towards the bathtub. 'No way I'm going to take a shower in there.' He came a little closer and eyed my work. 'Then again, it's good for use now.'

'Thank you. I take it you haven't been staying here?'

'Good grief, no. With the kitchen still empty and the bathroom that dirty? I had my things delivered the day before yesterday, hooked up the wifi, did some work, played the violin to check the acoustics – pointless, really, what with the furniture missing and all – and stayed over at Mycroft's.'

'Your what?'

'What do you mean, my what?'

'You said you were staying over at your–?'

'At my – oh!' He grinned. 'Mycroft. My brother.'

'That's an unusual name.'

'How many Sherlocks do you know?'

'The Jew in that Shakespeare play?'

'That's Shylock.'

'Oh. Right. So, you're going to stay at your brother's tonight, too?'

'I don't think so.' He looked around the bathroom. 'There's nothing left to be done in here.'

'You could have left a note. I had no idea you have a cleaning squad at your disposal.'

'I do not. I borrowed Mycroft's staff.'

'His… staff?' I echoed. 'What is he, a lord or something?'

Sherlock snorted. 'He's not. Although, sometimes I'm not so sure he knows that. Anyway, let me ring them up and cancel. Now that we're both here, we should be done in no time, right?'

'Well, I'm almost done in here.'

'I see that. When you're finished, you can help me unpack, yes?'

And he was out of the bathroom. I looked after him, shaking my head. If his brother had misgivings about being a lord, then what did that make Sherlock? Little Lord Fauntleroy? *When you're finished help me unpack* indeed.

But I did, in the end. Help him unpack. Watching him take his things out of the boxes one by one and look at them as he wandered around the living room got me all fidgety. Had he never moved house before?

'Mainly into partly furnished apartments,' he said when I asked him. 'Mycroft takes care of organisational stuff, you know, has my things packed and unpacked.'

'I see. And did he arrange for you to look at this flat, too?'

'He didn't. I'd been thinking about moving out of my last apartment for a while – they didn't like me playing my violin, you see – and when I mentioned as much to Tony, he said a friend of his mother's was renting out a flat on Baker Street, and here we are.'

He looked rather pleased with himself and for a brief moment I wondered whether I'd just moved in with somebody who'd lived under professional supervision until very recently. I shooed that thought aside because Tony would certainly have dropped a hint, but all he had said was "eccentric" and "a bit of a loner." Besides, Sherlock had signed the lease himself, with only Mrs Hudson and me around and no supervisor in sight. Maybe that lordly brother of his had merely exaggerated the pampering.

'Here we are,' I said in reply to his last remark. 'Let's get the rest of your boxes unpacked, shall we?'

Turned out a nudge was all he needed to get going – not a princeling after all – and when we had moved the sideboard against one wall and the shelves against the other and all of Sherlock's boxes were finally unpacked, our living room looked like a real living room and it wouldn't be long before it looked homey, too.

'Are you all set in your bedroom?' I asked. 'Or do you need help with anything up there?'

'No, I'm done. I put my suits and some of my shirts into your wardrobe, like we said.'

'I saw that.'

'Do you mind?'

'No, it's okay. I just hadn't taken you to be a suit kind of person.'

'I'm not. But I find them useful in my line of work.'

'And what is that?'

'I'm a consultant,' he replied, a little evasively.

So I hadn't been all wrong. 'Really? A consultant for what?'

'For people in need of a consultant. Really, John, it's a lot less intriguing than it may sound. Do you want to see my room?'

'Sure.'

His room was bigger than I remembered, only a little smaller than mine but offered a lot less storage space because of the slanting roof. The queen-size bed was made but had obviously not been slept in. On it lay a couple of folders and what looked like martial arts equipment, and two boxes stood on the side of the bed facing the wall. One box was open and seemed to contain more folders.

The low wardrobe stood half open and showed the rest of Sherlock's clothes – jeans, trousers, shirts, jumpers. And shoes. Lots of shoes. More shoes than I had owned in my entire life.

'Wow,' I said, impressed. 'That's a lot of clothes.'

'You think so?' He shrugged. 'Clothes maketh man.'

'I thought it was 'manners maketh man'.'

'That, too.' He closed his wardrobe. 'May I see your room?'

'Of course.'

He followed me downstairs. 'Now that's what I call a very neatly made bed. If I flip a coin on it, will it spring up again?'

'Probably.'

'How long have you been in the military?' He opened my wardrobe and inspected its contents. 'Did you use a ruler to arrange your stuff like that?'

'I don't need one. Years of training, I guess. And I served for nine years.'

He gave a low whistle and closed the wardrobe. 'Nine years. That's a long time.'

I shrugged. 'Didn't seem like a long time. I liked it.'

'Why did you leave?'

'Got injured.'

'That's right, your knee. I remember.'

'And lower leg. Not fit for active duty any longer.'

'Do you miss it?'

'Sometimes, yeah.'

'Are those the guinea pigs?' He walked over to the corner where the cage stood and crouched down. 'Where are they?'

'In hiding.' I crouched down next to him and opened the cage. 'Hey you two, meet your new flatmate.' I lifted the wooden house. Two sets of eyes stared up at us.

'They're a bit like fat rats,' Sherlock observed. 'Do they do any tricks?'

'Careful, you're hurting their feelings,' I said and put the house back. 'No tricks.'

'Boring.'

'That's what I thought, too. But they grow on you.'

'They do? How?'

'They're fun little critters. Cute, too. They're easy pets to have. You don't have to walk them and there's no furballs.'

'Mhm.' He didn't look convinced.

'Don't worry, they're my responsibility. You won't have to look after them.'

I rose and winced when my leg protested. Hauling furniture and boxes, running up and down the stairs and spending too much time in a crouching position were not among the recommended activities for artificial knees and semi-reconstructed shinbones.

Sherlock, on the other hand, rose from his crouch with an ease I envied.

'Can I teach them tricks?'

'You can try,' I said, a little dubiously. 'But give them time to get to know you, okay?'

'Of course.'

'I'm hungry. How about you? Have you eaten?'

'I haven't, but I'm not hungry. I need to get some work done.'

'All right. I think I saw a Thai takeaway around the corner. Want me to get you something for later?'

'No, thank you. I'll be upstairs.'

I looked after him as he vanished through the door and up to his bedroom, then reached for my wallet and my jacket with a sigh. Guess I was going to have my first dinner at 221B Baker Street all by myself.

Chapter Five

About two weeks after we had moved into our new flat, I met Sherlock's brother Mycroft who dropped by for a courtesy call. Or to inspect the premises. Probably the latter.

When I unlocked the door to our flat, I saw the lights in the living room were on, and the smell of Sherlock's favourite tea greeted me.

'Sherlock, do you think – oh.' I stopped. 'I had no idea you had a visitor. I'm sorry for barging in like that.'

A tall, portly man in an impeccable charcoal three-piece suit stood next to one of the armchairs, looking like he was about to leave.

'You must be Dr Watson,' he greeted me and extended his hand. 'Pleased to make your acquaintance. I'm Mycroft Holmes. How do you do.'

'How do you do,' I shook his hand. 'Pleased to meet you, too.'

So this was Sherlock's brother. At first glance, he looked nothing like lanky Sherlock and not only because of the extra weight he carried. Mycroft's hair was a rich, almost-honey blond and impeccably cut, as opposed to Sherlock's unruly shock of light brown hair. His nose was long and slightly convex whereas Sherlock's was short and perfectly straight. But if you squinted a little, you could spot a certain resemblance, in the way they carried themselves and how their blue-and-grey eyes zoomed in on you. Mycroft's gaze was a bit cooler than Sherlock's but his lips quivered the same way when he found something amusing.

They quivered now and I wondered what amused him.

'How do you find life with my brother, Dr Watson?'

'We are still getting to know each other.'

'I see.' A smile flickered across his face. 'I like what you've done to the place. Only two weeks and already it looks like you've been here forever.' He cast a meaningful look to the sideboard where Sherlock had pinned his unopened letters down with a jack-knife.

'I'm glad you approve, Mycroft,' said Sherlock cheerfully. 'John's the domesticated one, and it's his doing that this place looks like home and not like a storage room.'

'You don't say,' Mycroft murmured. 'Please do refrain from stabbing a knife through the papers I just gave you.'

'I shall do my very best not to forget.'

They tossed a few more good-natured verbal darts back and forth, and I quickly came to realise there was genuine affection between the brothers, hidden between layers and layers of well-practised patronising and equally well-practiced banter. I guessed Mycroft to be maybe 10 years older than Sherlock, and the taking care of things aspect didn't strike me as all that overbearing anymore when seen from up close. I guessed it was only natural for an older sibling to want to watch over a younger one. It was something that didn't stop just because you grew older. In most cases, anyway.

When Mycroft left, he presented me with his business card.

'Please do call me if anything happens, Dr Watson,' he said. 'Your call will be patched through to my direct line, no matter the time.'

'Thank you, Mr Holmes. Let's hope I will not have to take you up on your offer and ring you up at an ungodly time of day.' I pocketed his card and fished for one of mine but didn't find any. 'I'm sorry but I must have forgotten my cards at the surgery.'

'Don't worry about that.' He paused, his hand on the door handle. 'One more thing.'

'Yes?'

'Please make sure he eats.'

'Working on it.'

He gave me one last scrutinising stare, nodded and let himself out.

I looked at Mycroft's card. Only his name and a mobile number were printed on it. I turned it around. No business address, no title. Was he a mystery consultant, too?

I walked back into the living room where Sherlock was tuning his violin.

'What did Mycroft mean by telling me I should make sure you eat?'

He shrugged one shoulder.

'Sherlock, is there something I should know?'

'John, I'm not suffering from an eating disorder, if that's what the doctor inside you is worried about. Mycroft has to sustain the equivalent of a small country. I do not.'

And with that, he launched into one of his warm-up routines. Conversation time was over.

AH, THE VIOLIN. THE FIRST time I heard him play in the middle of the night I all but shot up from my bed, startled and confused and unable to place the sounds I was hearing. Then, as my hearing booted up and connected with my brain, I recognised the caterwauling for what it was and yanked my bedroom door open.

And there he stood with his back to me, my flatmate, dressed in a ratty t-shirt and a pair of pyjama bottoms that sat dangerously low on his slim hips, gently swaying with the horrible piece he was playing. For a moment I was distracted by the outline of what looked like a very firm arse but then the bow started jumping across the strings, creating sounds I was not going to allow at – I glanced over at the clock above the fireplace – 2.35am.

'What the fuck do you think you're doing?' I snapped, loud enough to be heard over the fiddling.

With a calm that could have tested a saint's patience, Sherlock finished the sequence of notes bouncing about, lowered the bow and turned to look at me, violin still tucked under his chin.

'I'm playing the violin.'

'No shit.'

'You said some violin play wouldn't wake you up.'

'That was before you started playing bloody Beethoven.'

'John, please.' He lowered the violin, too. 'That wasn't Beethoven. I was playing the capriccio from Stravinsky's violin concer–'

'I honestly don't care, Sherlock. Play the fiddle at night if it makes you happy, but please play something that will not raise the dead. Or me, for that matter.'

'Like what?'

'I don't know. You're the musician. Play something pretty.'

'Pretty.' He made a face. 'Pretty is boring.'

'Soothing, then. Play me a lullaby. Think of something to serenade me back to sleep.'

He opened his mouth as if to say something, but I turned and padded back to my bedroom, unwilling to start an argument about music in the middle of the night. I crawled back into bed and pulled the blanket up.

It was silent for a couple of minutes and I was beginning to doze off when Sherlock started playing again.

I groaned and was just about to get up when – wait, I knew that piece. It was an old Welsh lullaby my Gran used to sing to me when I was a little boy. How could Sherlock possibly–? Nonsense. It had to be coincidence. No way Sherlock could know about Gran. I'd never spoken about her to him. Or had I?

Whatever. The song was lovely, Sherlock played it well, and the old magic worked as it had all these years ago. I was asleep within moments.

Chapter Six

My night ended with the buzzing of my mobile phone. I reached for it, hoping it was not the surgery. I was not in the mood for an early morning emergency, but it wasn't work.

Halabi, K was calling.

'*Salaam*, my brother,' I said and rubbed a hand across my face. 'Why are you calling in the middle of the night? Or are you in a different time zone?'

'Heathrow. On the way to Dubai, then off to Hong Kong.' Karim's voice was typically gruff. I grinned. Not only did my London born-and-bred friend never waste time on niceties, early morning conversations ranked high among the top five things he hated.

'London time, then. Are you waking me up to share your travel plans?'

He grunted. 'I'm ringing in to ask if you want to meet for a pint when I get back.'

'Sure,' I said. 'And when would that be?'

'How about Wednesday next week?'

'Sounds good, I think.'

'You think?'

'Well, my schedule isn't as fully booked as yours. Unless I'm stuck at the operating table my evenings are fairly flexible.'

He snorted. 'Must be hard, being a doctor.'

'It helps pay the rent.'

'That dump's not worth the rent you pay.'

'Ah, but I've moved to Baker Street. Remember I asked you to help but you were conveniently sent on a business trip?'

'That's right, you moved. I was working on the Indian transaction then, wasn't I?'

'No idea.'

'No, I think it was the Korean deal. Bad timing, in any case. So, Marylebone, eh?' He whistled. 'Have you gone private with your work then?'

'No, still the same practice.'

'Won the lottery?'

'Flat-share.'

'I see. Cute flatmate?'

'Mhm,' I responded evasively.

'John, my brother, it really is about time we meet. Wednesday it is. Around 7pm?'

'Affirmative.'

'The *Broken Drum*?'

'Where else?'

'Excellent. Next week then, *inshallah*.'

'*Inshallah* indeed. Make sure you set yourself a reminder, yeah?'

He laughed and disconnected. I yawned, put the phone back on the bedside table, switched off the alarm clock that would go off any minute, and got up. After brushing my teeth I walked over to one of the living room windows, opened it, and looked outside. The sky was clear, and the air was fresh and crisp. Perfect for a morning run. I went back into my bedroom to change, then fetched my running shoes.

'Morning, John.'

Sherlock stood at the top of his chicken ladder and peered down at where I was going through my playlists, trying to make up my mind about which one to listen to.

'Morning, Sherlock.'

'Where are you going?'

'For a run. Care to join me?'

He scratched his head. 'Regent's Park?'

'Why not. The lakeside loop is just right. You up for it?'

'Give me three minutes.'

'You may have four. I'll do some stretching in the meantime.'

He joined me a few minutes later, wearing a pair of loose trousers and a faded Ramones shirt that either was child-sized or had suffered in the washing machine. It looked good on him, actually, bringing out his lean frame to full advantage. He bounced on his soles, did a number of squats and then bent over with his long legs spread wide and touched his palms to the floor.

Naturally I chose that exact moment to look up from what I was doing and damn near lost my balance.

'Careful, John!' He placed a steadying hand on my arm. 'What are you doing?'

Looking at your arse, Sherlock.

'Nothing to worry about,' I said, somewhat hastily. 'Wasn't paying attention for a moment. Let's go.'

His eyes held mine for a few heartbeats, and it was there and then when I realised that not only had he found me out, he shared my preference. I'm not much of a believer in gaydar and all that, but there's things you just recognise. Like, whether there's potential for more than just friendship. A mutual interest. And I thought I'd seen just that. *Huh.*

One corner of his mouth lifted and he nodded.

'Ready when you are.'

We jogged across the street and over to Regent's Park at a leisurely pace. Sherlock adapted his somewhat longer strides to mine, and we soon fell into a rhythm that suited us both. We were at about the same level of physical fitness, and, like me, he seemed to prefer running in silence, too. He interrupted the silence only once to ask about my leg.

'I thought running was off limits for people with artificial knees.'

'Oh, the knee isn't the problem,' I said. 'It's the lower leg I need to watch out for. Most of the time it's okay, it's only when it gets cold and wet or when I overwork the leg that it starts hurting. But I have both checked once a year, just to be safe.'

'Anything else you do, sports-wise?'

'Swimming, whenever I can. Gym, two or three times a week. And my bike. You?'

'Kendo.'

'So that's what all that stuff is. I thought it look martial artsy.'

'You could have just asked me, John.'

'I guess so. You been doing this long?'

'I started when I was 16-years-old.'

A group of retirees walking their dogs made us split up for a couple of metres.

'I used to practice archery with my brother,' he continued when we had the path to ourselves again. 'But his job eats up most of his time and we only get to shoot some arrows three, maybe four times a year.'

'Really?' I asked, surprised. 'He doesn't look the athletic type.'

'Don't underestimate him,' Sherlock said. 'He's pretty good with bow and arrow and he wasn't always that fat. He used to be in the military, too, so maybe one day the two of you can trade war stories.'

'Seriously?'

'Seriously.'

We finished our run in silence and walked up the stairs to our flat.

'You shower first,' he said. 'There's something I need to look into.'

'Thanks. Will you join me for breakfast?'

'I don't – ah, why not. Otherwise you'll tell Mycroft I'm starving myself.'

'That's right, I will. I'll set up the table when I'm done.'

But when I got out of the bathroom, I was greeted by the smell of coffee, and Sherlock was sitting in his preferred armchair, focussed on his tablet with his legs pulled up and his elbows sticking out, looking very much like a lanky teenager.

'Thanks for making coffee,' I said. 'I really need a cup.'

He looked up. 'Thought so,' he replied and let his eyes travel along my body, making me feel like a bug under a microscope. 'Did you wrestle at uni?'

'Rugby. Number eight position, if you're interested.'

'Ah,' he said and turned his focus back to his tablet. 'Bring me a cup, will you? Black, three sugars. Thanks.'

'Of course, dear.'

He looked up at that but didn't say anything, and I went to fetch coffee for us both.

So he liked blokes, Sherlock did. And he liked to run. I filed both away for later use, hoping that getting him to join me for the latter might...well. We'd see about that.

Chapter Seven

Sherlock did join me for another morning run later that week. And again. And again, until it became a much-beloved habit. For me, at least. At that point I wasn't too sure about Sherlock, but the fact that I heard his bedroom door open whenever I left the bathroom to change into my running gear gave me reason to hope that he was enjoying our exercise routine as much as I did.

We usually ran for about 30 to 45 minutes, depending on the weather and on whether or not it was a good leg day for me, but we always moved in perfect synchronicity with each other, either in companionable silence or chatting easily.

It was during one of our runs that I got my first insight into what Sherlock did for a living. I'd seen papers and photos lying around but he always made a point of hastily collecting them as soon as I got in, just as if I'd caught him brooding over state secrets.

'When do you have to be at the practice?' he asked.

'About half nine,' I said. 'I got a post surgery check-up scheduled for 10am and I need to prepare my room.'

'Don't your assistants do that for you?'

'I'm not your lordly brother,' I said. 'Our assistants and practice nurses have their hands full already. Besides, I rather like getting everything ready myself. Puts me in the right spirit.'

'And caters to your perfectionism, right?'

'How do you mean?'

'I mean that everything has to be just so, at least where basic organisation is concerned.'

'Are you telling me I'm a neat freak?'

'Neat, yes. Freak, I don't think so. I've watched you closely over the last couple of weeks–'

'Now who's the freak here?'

'But I think,' he continued, ignoring my words, 'it's to do with your military background. Some things just stick, eh? Anyway, I'd like to show you something.'

'Show me what?'

'You'll see.'

He steered me out of Regent's Park and towards Ulster Terrace where he hailed a cab. We drove for about 40 minutes, with him typing away on his ever present phone and not speaking until we stopped before a building I knew well enough.

'What on earth are we doing at the Royal London?' I asked, climbing out of the cab behind him.

He paid the cabbie and motioned for me to follow him. 'I need to ask your advice.'

'My advice on what?'

'I'm missing one minor detail on something I'm working on. I'm almost there, I can feel it, but there's one tiny thing that I can't quite identify.'

What was he getting at? And why were we–

'Are you taking me to the morgue?' I asked, recognising the route he was taking.

'I am, yes.'

When we turned the last corner, the nurse in attendance didn't seem particularly surprised to see him.

'Morning, Sherlock,' the sturdy young man said. 'Brought a friend?'

'A trained pair of eyes. John, Rafi, Rafi, Dr Watson. Where is he?'

'Number 3017.'

'Thanks.'

I hated morgues. I truly, deeply did. I'd seen my share of patients for whom all help came too late and whose lifeless bodies I'd had to send to the morgue, both during my time in the military and during my time as trauma surgeon. Sometimes even your very best isn't good enough, and it's something you never, ever get used to. So, yeah, a morgue was not much of a favourite place of mine. Never has been, never will be.

Sherlock, in blissful ignorance of my musings, walked up to the storage unit and pulled out a drawer. On it lay the dead body of a young man who looked to have been in his mid-20s.

'Come here, John,' Sherlock said and I joined him.

He pointed at three slash wounds. 'See this? The chest and upper arm wound wouldn't have caused his death but this here,' he indicated the carotid artery, 'this was unstoppable.

'Problem is, I have no idea what weapon may have caused this, and neither does the pathologist. Something small and serrated but we've not been able to figure out what kind of knife causes wounds like these.'

'Too blunt for a knife,' I said and stared into the young man's face for a moment, then looked for and found a box of rubber gloves. I snapped a pair on, then hesitated.

'I'm not sure if I should be doing this,' I said, to no-one in particular.

Rafi nodded encouragingly. 'S'all right, mate, Sherlock already signed you in, yesterday, and Dr Muller authorised it.'

I shot Sherlock a sharp glance. He smiled and winked, and so I bent forward to inspect the body.

The deceased had been in good physical shape and of an average, unremarkable build. The body was slim with no excessive body fat and his muscles weren't particularly defined. There were a few scars, small ones, stitched together expertly, no signs of drug abuse. His lower lip was split and his right cheekbone was bruised.

Rafi helped me turn him on his side so I could look at the young man's back and the back of his legs, too. Nothing noticeable there. The only eye-catcher was a tattoo between his shoulder-blades depicting the logo of a Premier League football team.

We rolled him back and when I nodded, Rafi covered the man's body once more and pushed the drawer back. I binned the gloves.

'He was a football fan, wasn't he?' I asked. It was more of a rhetorical question, given the tattoo, and Sherlock didn't bother answering. 'Where was he found?'

'Near Selhurst Park Stadium. In the parking lot of a car cosmetic specialist on Clifton Road.'

'After a game?'

'Yes.'

I pursed my lips, thinking. I was well familiar with how football games sometimes went, or rather: ended. I stitched young (and sometimes not so young) hotheads together on a regular basis, splinted broken bones where possible, fixed dislocated shoulders, you name it. Why football brought out such violence amongst its fans was beyond me; I'd never seen anything like that after a rugby game. But that's a whole different subject and doesn't belong here.

Most injuries I'd looked after had been caused by fists, booted feet, clubs, even brass knuckles on more than one occasion. Knives, too, although carrying weapons into a stadium wasn't as easy as it used to be, with security having been enhanced. Unless–

'Keys,' I said. 'The wounds were caused by keys.'

I took my keys out of my pocket and positioned them so that one key blade pointed out between my thumb and index finger and the blades of the second and third key extended out of the bottom of my hand. 'See? You can slash like this,' I demonstrated, 'or stab with the bottom ones like this.'

Sherlock looked at me and nodded solemnly, as if I had just proven a point.

'I knew it,' he said, satisfied. 'I knew you'd see it.' He turned to Rafi and held out his hand. 'I told you, didn't I? You owe me a twenty.'

I looked from Sherlock to Rafi and back to Sherlock.

'What?' I asked, incredulous. 'You already knew the answer?'

Sherlock inclined his head.

'Was that a pub quiz to test me?'

'Yes,' my flatmate replied cheerfully and pocketed his winnings. 'Of course I knew about the keys, and, yes, I wanted see whether it's really so hard to find out. Most people look, but they don't observe. They see many things, but fail to connect the dots. It pleases me that you seem to at least grasp the basics of proper deduction.'

'Thank you, Sherlock. I feel so much better now. Mind telling me why you're allowed to come and go as you please and how on earth you're authorised to sign people in to look at a dead body?'

'He comes here all the time,' Rafi said, sorting through a pile of paperwork. 'Dr Muller likes him, and he usually comes with–'

'That's quite enough, Rafi,' Sherlock interrupted him. 'I've kept John for long enough. He still needs to shower and breakfast before he can be let loose on his own patients. He works with people who are still alive and we'd like to keep it that way.'

With that, he placed a hand on the small of my back and pushed me towards the exit.

'Tell Dr Muller I'll stop by again later today to collect the samples he promised me.'

'Will do. Bye, Sherlock. Bye, Dr Watson.'

SHERLOCK HOPPED OUT OF the cab a few minutes away from home.

'I'll pick up breakfast for you,' he said. 'You go shower and all, and it'll be ready for you when you're done.'

'Why would you do that?'

'You won me twenty quid. It's only fair to share, right?'

'See you–' I began but he'd already slammed the door shut. I looked after him, shaking my head and wondering what all this had been about. And what kind of samples could he possibly want from a pathologist?

Maybe not the best thing to think about, given that he'd just wandered off to get breakfast. I'd probably find out soon enough.

CHAPTER EIGHT

'SHERLOCK?'

Not a sound came from the upstairs bedroom so I tried again, louder this time.

'Sherlock!'

No reply.

'What did you do with the guinea pig food?'

Silence. Then, 'Fridge.'

'Not the veggies. The pellets.'

'Freezer.'

'What?'

'Freezer.'

The hell? I opened the freezer. There was a big container crammed in between packages of frozen pizzas and ice-cream that hadn't been there yesterday. It was heavy, and I struggled to get it out without pulling everything else out with it. It had '*Thomas 09/03*' handwritten on it, and I carefully lifted the lid.

And immediately closed it again.

'Sherlock!' I yelled. 'Come down here at once!'

The upstairs door opened. I heard footsteps tapping down the chicken ladder and Sherlock appeared in the kitchen door, dishevelled and bedheaded.

'Why are there eyeballs frozen in what looks like liquefied guinea pig pellets?'

He scratched his head. 'I wanted to find out what a mixture of pressed vegetable-and-hay pellets and balsamic vinegar will do to human eye tissue.'

'These are actual human eyes?'

'Of course they are.'

'Do I want to know where you got them? Wait – are these the samples your pathologist friend promised you?'

'Dr Muller. Yes.' He took the container out of my hands. 'But before you even ask, I don't intend to keep them. I – borrowed them.'

'You borrowed human eyeballs,' I repeated, stunned. 'May I ask what for?'

'An experiment,' he said and put the offending container back into the freezer.

'This will not go in there,' I snapped and pulled it out again. 'For fuck's sake, Sherlock, that's where we keep our food! I'll have to throw everything away and scrub and sterilise the whole thing, and thank you very much for that.'

'Don't be ridiculous, John. Nothing's been contaminated. I always make sure the containers are properly closed.'

'Are you telling me there's more in there?'

He shrugged. 'I'm fairly certain I've returned everything.'

'You're fairly–' Oh, but that was disgusting.

I ripped the door open and did a quick inventory check but there was nothing there that didn't belong. I sighed. 'And what should I give poor Bodie and Doyle for their breakfast now? Hm?'

'There's still greens in the fridge,' Sherlock pointed out. 'They won't starve. I'll look after them.'

'I was afraid you would say that. They're herbivores, Sherlock, vegetarians. No scrambled eggs or leftover sausages for them.'

'We'll share a bowl of cereal.'

'You will do no such–'

He raised his hands in a gesture of peace. 'Got it. Greens for the boys, cornflakes for me. Yes?'

I narrowed my eyes. 'And no shaving their behinds again.'

'I swear.'

'No shaving them anywhere.'

'Promise.'

I sighed again. 'Here,' I held the container out to him and he obediently reached for it. 'Please return the eyeballs to wherever you got them and throw the container away. I'll scrub the freezer when I get home.'

'What about the fridge?'

'What about it?'

'Nothing.'

'Sherlock!'

'Really, nothing, just kidding, John. Kidding,' he repeated when I yanked the fridge door open. 'There's nothing in there that doesn't belong.'

'You sure? Crickets and mealworms all gone?'

That had been my introduction to Sherlock's "experiments". Crickets and mealworms neatly stacked between cheese and butter. Not much of an appetiser but nowhere near in the range of human eyeballs and vinegar.

Sherlock didn't grace me with a reply, pressed the container against his chest and made for the bathroom. Good thing I was already done in there. I would hate to take a shower with a couple of eyeballs checking me out.

'Promise you will eat breakfast, Sherlock,' I shouted after him. A grunt was all I got so I started the coffee maker, chopped some cucumber and lettuce into a heavy stoneware bowl and went to feed the boys.

'Sorry there'll be no crunchies today,' I informed them. 'Uncle Sherlock has seen fit to use your food for one of his experiments.'

I QUICKLY FORGOT ALL ABOUT eyeballs when I arrived at the surgery. An outbreak of scarlet fever in a nearby preschool sent a flock of children our way, with more than a few parents showing the tell-tale symptoms of pink-red rashes and coated tongues as well, and we had our hands full. When I finally got out, it was past seven, and I was going to be late for my pub date with Karim. But as Karim was hardly ever punctual, I didn't try to outrun time.

And just as I had expected, there was no sign of him when I finally arrived at the *Broken Drum*, so I got a pint of Irish Red and settled into our favourite corner. I was used to waiting for Karim. Always working, always late. He'd been that way back in our uni days and it had very nearly cost him his fly-half position, but only nearly. He'd been too good a fly-half to be kicked off the rugby team, and besides, he'd never been late for a game.

It was 7.45pm. I pulled out my phone and dialled his number. He answered after the second ring.

'John, I forgot,' he said in lieu of a greeting.

'So I've noticed,' I replied. 'I'm half way through my first Irish Red already. Any chance of seeing you tonight?'

'I'm so sorry but I can't make it. I'm off to Dubai again tomorrow for the final round of negotiations. I've been crunching numbers since yesterday. It's touch and go–'

Silence.

'Karim? You still there?'

Heavy breathing.

'Karim?'

'The *fuck* is that?'

'What is what?' I asked, alarmed.

Something crashed at the other end and I jumped. Then a stream of Arabic flooded the ether and I wondered if it contained any trigger words that would make MI5 trace down our line.

'Fuck this shit,' Karim finally said. 'I'll swing by for a pint, if you're willing to wait for another 15 or so.'

'No problem. Want me to get something for you?'

'Get me a pint of Erdinger, will you?'

'Sure.'

We rang off and I went to the bar to order Karim's Erdinger and another Red for me.

Less than 10 minutes later a wiry man in a rumpled grey suit made a beeline from the pub's entrance straight to where I was sitting, as if he was pulled in by a gossamer thread.

'Beer,' he greeted me and reached for his pint. 'You are a lifesaver, my brother.'

'Hello, Karim. Did you fly here or what?'

He did not grace me with a reply and greedily gulped down half his pint.

'Ah, that's better,' he sighed and put down his glass. 'Nothing like some good German brew to restore your faith in good.'

'Easy on the strong stuff. You know German beer is no laughing matter.'

Karim peered across the table with a faint look of alarm on his face and I laughed.

'I'm joking. It's alcohol-free.'

'You had me nervous for a sec.'

'I couldn't resist. That's for keeping me waiting. What on earth happened?'

He arched one of his mobile eyebrows. 'You don't want to know, John. Be grateful you decided to go to medical school and do something useful with your life.'

'I am. I wouldn't want your job for all the money in the world,' I said, and I meant it. Karim worked at some international investment bank and while his salary was indecent, so were his working hours. Barely any free time, 24-7 availability for his clients who sat all over the world in all kinds of time zones. But he loved it, work animal that he was.

'Let's just say I'm working on a massive deal. If this goes as planned, they'll make me senior director.'

'And that means what?'

'New business cards,' he said, grinning. 'And another layer on my annual bonus.' He fished for one of the stools and climbed on it.

'Man, I have so much to tell you but I'll have to stick to the headlines tonight. I must get back in about 20 minutes. My spreadsheet froze and crashed Excel while we were on the phone and I'll have to double-check everything I've worked on to make sure the references are still in place. The yield assumption is a dog, and I really need to smooth over the five-year projection or else there'll be no signing on Friday.'

'And pop goes the bonus.'

'Exactly so.' He took another swig. 'Something odd's popped up in one of my calculations, and I wonder if it's reflected in the agreement's attachments.'

'What are you talking about?'

'Never mind. Let's not waste our time on deals and stuff. How's that flat-share of yours coming along?'

'It's...interesting,' I said.

'Oh yeah? Interesting in what sense?'

'I don't even know where to begin.'

'Like your new place?'

'Very much.'

'Your rats still around?'

'Yes. And they're guinea pigs, not rats.'

'Allah, how old do they get?' He rolled his eyes. 'Nice flatmate?'

'Define nice.'

'Agreeable manners?'

Now I rolled my eyes. 'Next.'

'Pretty?'

'Not pretty, no.'

'Boring?'

'Anything but.'

'So he's hot.'

'What makes you say that?'

He spread his hands. 'You were hesitant at pretty and quick at anything but. Do you have a photo?'

'Nope, sorry.'

'Shame. So. Hot without manners, eh.'

'Not entirely without manners.'

'Uh-huh. What does he do? For a living, I mean.'

'I don't really know.'

'Eh? You live together, don't you? Haven't you thought to ask him?'

I shrugged. 'I have asked him, once or twice, but he's never really replied. I think he's a private detective of sorts or perhaps a crime journalist. There's always reports and photos lying around, and he comes and goes at the weirdest hours. He took me to the morgue at the Royal London the other day to ask my advice on something he already knew. Lord, and some of the stuff he does…'

And before I knew it, I told him about the visit to the morgue and the eyeballs in the freezer, about Sherlock's horrible eating habits, about the nightly violin play–

Karim held up a finger. 'What was that about playing the violin?'

'He plays very well, like he's been classically trained.'

'That's not what I meant. You said the music helps you fall asleep. Are you telling me he starts playing when you go to bed? Like a sleep timer on your radio?'

'No.' I frowned. Sherlock hardly ever played the violin around the time I usually went to bed. He played in the middle of the night after I–

'You know,' I slowly said, 'before you asked me that I would have said I wake up from his play. But you know what? I think he only starts playing after I've woken up. Apart from that first time, that is. I woke up from that.'

'Aha.'

'What?'

'Tell me, John, do you still have nightmares?'

'Yes, but they're not so bad anymore and less often.'

'But you still have them?'

'I do. What does this have to do – oh.' I looked at him. 'You think he hears me?'

Karim snorted. 'It's hard not to hear you when you're having bad dreams.'

'But I–'

I fell silent. Was it still so bad? I didn't think so. I'd been haunted by nightmares ever since I got back from my last tour in Afghanistan, after I got injured, but I'd been through extensive therapy since then, both physical and psychological, and my dreams didn't haunt me as much these days as they had back then. Or did they?

'John, you stayed with me for a month after your release from hospital. It was bad, believe me. You woke up screaming almost every bloody night. Very near gave me a heart attack, brother.'

'But I don't wake up screaming anymore.'

'You sure?'

'Yes. I used to wake up from my own screams. Now I just – I just wake up.'

'So maybe – uhm, what's his name again?'

'Sherlock.'

'What kind of name is that? Isn't that the Jewish merchant in the Shakespeare play?'

'That's Shylock.'

'Oh. Right. Is it possible Sherlock hears you and plays all these soft melodies to help you fall asleep again?'

'You think so?'

He shrugged. 'Why not? If he's as perceptive as you say, then maybe it's his way of looking after you. Like you're probably already mother-henning him.'

'Hey.'

'Shut up. Again, you stayed with me for a month. You were the patient and I was supposed to be looking after you. But you were the one fussing over me, remember? Cleaning up, cooking, making sure I eat, preparing lunch boxes for me.'

'I did not.'

'Did too. Mother hen.'

I bit my lip. 'Am I that bad?'

'You're not. You care for those close to your heart. That's good. Nothing to be ashamed of.' He took another gulp. 'I'd like to meet him, your Sherlock. I have an idea we would get along just fine.'

'He's not my Sherlock.'

'Ah, but he will be.'

'We'll see about that.' Time to change the subject. 'Your turn. I have a feeling you're trying to hide something from me.'

He glanced at his watch.

'Oh no,' I said. 'You will tell me before you return to your fancy spreadsheets. What's been going on in your life since we last spoke?'

He lowered his gaze and his dark cheeks turned a shade darker.

'You met someone,' I said and when his lips split into a grin, I leaned over and punched his arm. 'When did you plan on telling me?'

'I was interested in what you had to say,' he defended himself. 'And your Sherlock sounds like he's a good one.'

'He's not my – you're a twat, Halabi, you know that?'

'I've been called worse.'

'So tell me. What's his name? What does he do? How old is he? Facts, my man, facts and figures.'

'His name's Djamal Mokhtari. He's originally from Marrakech but his family moved to London when he was 10-years-old and he has a British passport.'

'That's nice,' I said. 'You can tell me all about his family history when we have more time. How old? Job? What does he look like?'

'He's 38 and he's a linguist.'

'He's a what?'

'A linguist. Someone who has studied languages.'

'I know what a linguist is, Karim. Are you telling me you've fallen for a nerd?'

'Djamal's no nerd,' Karim bristled. 'We met at the gym.'

'A weightlifting nerd is still a nerd. Or does he do yoga? Please tell me you've not fallen for a yoga nerd.'

'What's wrong with yoga? You should try it some time, John.'

'I stretch enough, thank you.'

'Do you? Have you tried–'

'Tick-tock.'

'Bite me. Anyway, he's Moroccan, he's tall, he's smart, he's gorgeous. Want to see a photo?'

'Sure.'

Karim pulled his mobile out of his pocket, unlocked it and winced when he saw his message screen.

'Shit.'

He wiped the message screen away and pulled up his photo album, scrolled through an impressive collection of pictures and finally chose one.

'Here,' he said and handed me the phone. 'That's Djamal.'

A very handsome man smiled at me from the screen. Djamal looked younger than 38 and not like a language geek at all. Had Karim told me he was seeing a model, I would have believed him. A simple white t-shirt and a well-fitting pair of jeans on a lean, hard body – you can't do much better than that. Add dark, unruly curls, dark, laughing eyes, a proud aquiline nose and there's your fairy-tale heartthrob. Small wonder Karim had fallen hard for this nerd.

'Well done,' I said and handed the phone back to him. 'He really is gorgeous.'

'*Mashallah*,' Karim replied and pocketed his phone. 'He makes me happy, too.'

He checked the time.

'I must go back now but tell you what: when I come back from

Dubai, how about dinner? You, me, Djamal and Sherlock. What do you think?'

'Sounds good. When do you come back?'

'Friday. But we're already booked for the weekend. And the week will be a nightmare, what with final negotiations and such. How about the Saturday after that?'

'Not working for me. Ambulance service at a League Two game and an extra volunteer shift at the Royal London.'

He hummed and fished for his phone again. 'Tuesday?' he suggested after some scrolling.

'Tuesday's good,' I confirmed after some scrolling of my own.

'Excellent. I'll check back with Djamal and we'll think of a nice place to go.'

We both entered the dinner into our calendars and went outside. The third cab stopped, but before Karim got in, he pulled me into a fierce hug.

'I'm happy for you, John.'

'Why is that?'

'You look happy. And that makes me happy, too. I can't wait to meet him.'

I patted his back. 'Don't get too happy, my brother, or the cab will drive off without you.'

'See you in two weeks.'

'Best of luck with the number crunching, yeah?'

'Thanks. I need all the luck I can get.' He got into the cab, but before he closed the door, he gave me one last wave.

I waved back and watched the cab turn into Charing Cross Road, then went to the Underground station to catch the Bakerloo line home.

As I sat on the train, staring at my own reflection in the opposite window, I had to admit to myself that I envied Karim for his new-found happiness. Isn't that what we all want, to find someone to share our life with? I'd seen too much to still dream of a happily ever after, but I'd gladly take the happy for now.

Karim had said I looked happy, and while I didn't know about that, I sure was content. I liked having someone around to look after – although "mother hen" did take it a bit too far – and I'd come to look forward to coming home each day. Home to find Sherlock doing whatever he thought needed doing. I never quite knew what to expect the moment I opened the door, but I'd come to look forward to that, too.

And man, he was hot. He was nowhere near as good-looking as Djamal, but once you saw his attractiveness, you couldn't unsee it. I knew I couldn't. It was in his smile and the way the corners of his mouth turned upwards, the way his nose crinkled when he was laughing, the absent-minded way he brushed his hair back, how his blue-and-grey eyes turned from laser-sharp to water-colour sky.

Should I just make a move? I mean, what was I afraid of? We were grown men, were we not? And I was fairly certain he didn't dislike what he saw when he looked at me.

Risking our flatmate camaraderie, that's what I was afraid of.

Him not wanting me the way I wanted him, that's what I was afraid of even more.

Chapter Nine

'Do I have to?' Sherlock groaned. 'I'm in the middle of something.'

'Well, you don't have to, but it would mean a lot to me.'

'But I–'

'Please, Sherlock? Karim is like a brother to me, and I'd like very much for the two of you to meet.'

He made a face, heaved a theatrical sigh and unfolded his legs. 'All right, if it really is that important to you.'

'It is. Thank you.'

'Do I have to dress up? I don't want to wear a tie.'

'That won't be necessary. It's a decent restaurant but not too posh.'

'Got it. My Sunday best, then. Minus tie.'

'I really appreciate that. And don't worry, you'll get along well.'

'If you say so,' he muttered. 'How much time do I have?'

'You have two hours. The reservation is for eight o'clock. Will that be enough to get you into your Sunday best?'

He gave a reluctant grin and nodded. 'It'll do. Just don't expect any miracles.'

'You must be Djamal,' I greeted the tall man standing before the restaurant Karim had picked for our dinner. 'I'm sorry for keeping you waiting. I'm John Watson, and this is Sherlock Holmes.'

'I've only just arrived myself,' Djamal said and held out his hand. 'Good to finally meet you, John. Hello, Sherlock.'

'Djamal,' Sherlock shook hands with him, too.

'Karim will be a trifle late and asks to be apologised.' Djamal said. 'His clients have asked to be taken to the property they plan to invest in, and that has caused a massive delay.'

I raised my eyebrows. 'So what's new?'

Djamal laughed. 'He said you would understand.'

He was every bit as attractive as he had appeared in the photo Karim had shown me, if not more.

'Let's go inside,' he suggested. 'It's eight already and you know how they are at places like this.'

'You show up two minutes late and your table is gone.'

'Exactly.'

'I'm surprised he hasn't moved the dinner back yet another week,' I said as we sat down. 'Probably because Ramadan starts next week. Thursday, right?'

'Wednesday,' Djamal confirmed and accepted the menu the waitress handed him. 'I'm surprised you have the date in mind.'

I shrugged. 'Not that it matters much with Karim's work hours being what they are, but I've learnt to keep an eye out for Ramadan. He tends to use it as an apology to show up even later than usual and keeps forgetting that my work days start a lot earlier than his.'

'You're a doctor, yes? Do you have to work shifts?'

'John doesn't work shifts,' Sherlock answered for me. 'He's a trauma surgeon but works at a GP practice. He gets up at precisely six o'clock, goes for a run and comes back for a shower, a shave, and a quick breakfast, or heads straight for the gym, showers there and eats on the way to the practice. He doesn't shave on gym days.' He closed his menu. 'I usually join him for his runs but I don't do gym.'

'I don't particularly enjoy it either,' Djamal said. 'But I hurt my back pretty badly a few years ago and must stick to a somewhat regular workout routine.'

'What happened?' I asked.

'Motorcycle accident. Nothing dramatic, more an unhappy combination of poor judgement and stupidity. No-one got hurt but me. But it was in the gym where I met Karim so I guess it's not really that bad after all.'

We ordered our drinks and chatted commonplaces, sports and jobs. Well, Djamal and I were chatting. Sherlock was silent most of the time as if reluctant to give anything personal away and his eyes kept returning to his phone that sat next to his neatly folded napkin.

'What do you do, Sherlock?' Djamal asked when our drinks arrived, in what seemed a final and near-desperate effort to lure Sherlock into joining our conversation.

Sherlock looked up from his phone and shrugged a shoulder. 'Consulting work.'

'Really? And what kind of consulting work? Legal, banking, social work?'

'Consulting detective.'

'Like a private detective?'

Djamal sure wasn't easily discouraged. I wondered whether he would be graced with a proper reply. The trip to the morgue had shed some light on the nature of Sherlock's work but I was still mostly guessing when it came to the details. For whatever reason he didn't want to tell me, and I didn't want to prod.

Sherlock hesitated, but then he sighed. 'Not quite,' he said. 'I do accept private clients now and then, provided it's an interesting case.'

'So you work with the police?'

'On occasion, but not exclusively. Should we order now or should we wait for Karim?'

Well, so that was all the information we would get, obviously, and both Djamal and I reached for our mobiles. Sure as rain, there was a message from Karim saying the investors were still going on about the terms and conditions of the proposed investment, and he had no idea when he would be able to finally join us. Djamal and I shared a knowing look.

'Food,' I said and Sherlock signalled for the waitress to take our order.

Sherlock and Djamal both ordered a pasta dish, and I went for a steak with salad, but when our food finally arrived, Sherlock poked at his tagliatelle without much enthusiasm and returned to contributing little more than monosyllabic grunts to our conversation.

It wasn't hard to see why Karim had fallen for Djamal. It wasn't his good looks alone – yes, Karim liked his men beautiful – but if beauty was all they had to offer, he grew bored pretty quickly. Djamal was smart, witty and well-read. When he revealed he practised *razmafzah*, Persian martial arts, Sherlock snapped out of his self-imposed silence in the blink of an eye and engaged in a lively discussion on swords, sabres, and parrying techniques.

His pasta sat pushed aside with less than three or four bites eaten, and I frowned, Mycroft's word of warning still on my mind. 'Make sure he eats,' he had said, and so I reached over and swapped plates when Sherlock raised his hands to demonstrate a grip technique he favoured. His eyes were on Djamal and he didn't seem to be paying attention to what I was doing. At least he didn't acknowledge it.

'You see, you get a much better angle if you close your fingers around the hilt like this,' he said and made a sideways motion that had me duck out of the way.

'You certainly do,' Djamal said. 'But it's not going to work with crossguards. And definitely not on horse-back, either.'

'Crossguards, pah,' Sherlock made a dismissive sound, picked up his fork and knife, and cut into my steak. 'Personally, I find them overrated. Nothing beats a good, clean Japanese design. But you do have a point when it comes to mounted fighting. I hadn't thought of that.' He speared a piece of meat, as if to make a point, and nodded appreciatively. 'This really is a good steak,' he said, chewing. 'How do you like your pasta, John?'

Djamal looked up from his plate, surprised. So he seemed to have noticed the swap.

'Not bad,' I said. 'Just the right amount, too.'

I would have to run an extra mile tomorrow morning, what with that combination of cream and cheese, but watching Sherlock finish his – my – steak was well worth it.

Karim finally joined us when we were discussing dessert versus coffee.

'I am so dreadfully sorry,' he said as he took his seat next to Djamal. 'Same shit, different team. Some lowly servant's dinner plans don't mean squat when there's a multi million pound deal at stake. Would it be all right if I ordered something to eat? I had a bite during the meeting, but it was hardly enough to keep my stomach from rumbling too loudly.'

'Sure.' Djamal got up to fetch a menu for him, and Karim eyed Sherlock with open curiosity.

'I take it you're John's flatmate, yes?' he asked. 'So how do you like having his fat rats around? Stepped on one of them already?'

'Hey,' I protested. 'I will have no pet-shaming at this dinner table. You change the subject right now or I will have to ask you to leave.'

Karim held up a hand. 'What's there to pet-shame? They're noisy, they're all over the place and they shit everywhere.'

'They're not all over the place, and they do not shit everywhere.'

'They are, and they do,' Sherlock said with a grin. 'John cleans up behind them all the bloody time.'

'Ha.' Karim nodded, satisfied. 'Thought as much. Thanks,' he said, taking the menu Djamal had brought for him. 'Let's see.' He studied the starter selection with a frown.

'Anything you can recommend?'

'We skipped the starters,' I said.

He grunted and eyed my plate. 'And you had... Is that veggie pasta? The hell is wrong with you, John?'

'He swapped plates with Sherlock,' Djamal said.

Karim's eyebrows shot up and Sherlock gave me a surprised look. 'You did? I never noticed.' Sherlock sounded genuinely baffled.

'You didn't notice you started with pasta and ended with steak?'

asked Djamal and Karim, at the same time, 'You gave up your steak for pasta?'

I shrugged, and Karim gave me a long, hard stare but didn't say anything.

He finally ordered a combination of starter plates, not without some serious haggling that had Djamal rolling his eyes, but Sherlock encouraged him by suggesting an even more impossible combination that made the waitress's eyes shoot daggers at him.

An incoming call on Sherlock's phone ended the debate. He made a face as if now was an inconvenient time to disturb him, and why hadn't they called earlier when he was still bored, but excused himself nevertheless and took the call outside.

'I'm really sorry but I must go,' he said when he came back a few moments later. 'Something's come up with the case I'm working on, and my partner needs my help.'

'Your partner?' I asked, surprised. I'd somehow thought he was working alone.

'Strictly speaking she's my client. Or more precisely, the representative of my actual client. But we've worked so many cases together that I've started to consider her more of a partner than a client.'

'I see. Well, I guess if you must go then you must go.'

'Apologies.' He nodded towards Karim and Djamal. 'Good meeting you. Maybe some other time.'

'I'm sure there'll be plenty of occasions,' Karim said. 'I still need to inspect your place.'

'That's right,' I said. 'You've not been there yet.'

'See? So we'll see each other soon, *inshallah*. Good luck with your case, Sherlock.'

'No luck needed. I already know where she's stuck. Later, John.'

'Later. Be safe.'

Karim looked after Sherlock, then turned to me with a grin.

'Hot,' he said.

'Quiet.'

His grin grew wider. 'I have yet to see you give up a good piece of meat for me.'

'That's because you usually order half a cow for yourself.'

'You won't wiggle out of this one, my man. You fancy him.'

'Jealous?'

'No. All I ever wanted is sitting right here beside me.' He gave Djamal's hand a quick squeeze.

'So how did the meeting go?' I asked. 'Ready to order your new business cards?'

'Don't jinx it,' he warned me. 'But yes, it's looking good so far. I drowned them in analyses and projections, and they were duly impressed with the site, too.'

'I didn't expect to hear otherwise.'

His drink arrived and we toasted each other.

'To growing up and settling down,' he said and clinked glasses with me. 'About time, too.'

I didn't reply and took a swig.

Karim winked at me and sat his glass down. 'Remember when we met at the *Broken Drum* and I said there was something odd about my calculations?'

'You mean when you went ape shit on the phone and had me scared about being hunted down by some anti-terror squad?'

'I did yell a little, didn't I.'

'That's one way of putting it, yeah.'

'You mean he made your eardrum explode?' Djamal suggested.

'I see you've already encountered the Halabi wrath.'

'Not directed towards me, but, yes, I've noticed a tendency to swear.'

'Better get used to it.'

'Sitting right here,' Karim said, waving his hand between us. 'Don't you dare team up and go parental. I'm used to John being my surrogate mother. Don't you join him, *albi*.'

'Sorry, love.' Djamal lowered his eyes but grinned.

'Anyway, looks as if someone is running a side business but did a piss poor job encrypting their files. It all got entangled with the reference codes of my calculation and fucked my whole model up.'

'And what would that be, that side job?'

'I can't tell you.'

'Can't or won't?'

'Can't. And wouldn't, even if I could. You know that. But it certainly doesn't belong in the investment opportunity folder. I shot off a quick mail to our CIO to have it checked, in case anyone's been messing with our drives.'

'Heard anything back yet?'

'Nah, just sent it before I went into the meeting. Ah,' he beamed at the waitress, 'here comes my lifesaver. Thank you so very much, this looks fantastic.'

'Enjoy your meal,' she said, her professional smile back in place. 'May I bring anything else?'

I shook my head. 'Not for me, thank you.'

'I'll have an espresso, please,' Djamal said.

She nodded and vanished.

Karim dug in like a starving man and only paused to ask Djamal to check for the exact date of their next *Star Wars* watch-a-thon.

'You and Sherlock are most welcome to join us,' he said. 'We'll be six, plus the two of you. We'll spread out on the floor, Bedouin-style, you know, cushions and all. Come on, it'll be fun.'

'That's all eight *Star Wars* films plus *Rogue One*, yes?'

'Which part of watch-a-thon didn't you understand?'

'Thanks but no thanks. You know damn well I hate the prequel trilogy.'

'That's because you don't understand the impact they have on things that are to come.' Karim turned to Djamal. 'I hate to break it to you, with you two just having bonded and all, but dear John here used to prefer *Star Trek* when we first met.'

Djamal drew a hissing breath and gave me a reproachful look. Karim nodded gravely.

'That's right. He used to think the *Enterprise* was a cooler ship than the *Falcon,* but I showed him the light. Sadly, he still slips and comes up with shit like, *ah, but the prequels suck.*'

'We will work on this,' Djamal said in a determined voice. 'Do you know where Sherlock stands on the matter?'

'I've not yet discussed it with him.'

'What?' Karim lowered his fork and mock-glared at me.

'Forgive me,' I said in what I hoped was a meek voice.

'You have just confirmed your attendance. Sherlock is free to decide but you better be there. So, which weekend did we say?'

'It's the weekend after your team-building event,' Djamal said after some scrolling.

'Team-building?' I asked. 'Abseiling, kayaking and shit?'

Karim made a face. 'I wish it was abseiling. At least I'd get to do something physical. Nope, it's going to be a weekend of fun and in-depth analysis,' he said between bites. 'Laser-tag and psycho babble. Where do we stand, what can the individual contribute to achieve the company goals, gimme a T, gimme an I and so forth.'

'Fuck me,' I said sympathetically. 'I pity you.'

'Thank you. They've scheduled it for the first weekend after Ramadan to make sure we can all attend and not faint in the process, you know, us Muslims being starved and dehydrated and all.'

'How thoughtful.'

'Isn't it. Well, that gives you some six weeks to prepare. And don't you dare come up with weak-arsed excuses of volunteer work at some football game or the trauma surgery where you like to hang out when you have nothing else to bloody do.'

'Look who's talking: pot, kettle! Just so you know, I've cut down my volunteer work.'

'Oh yeah? Since when?'

'Since I've moved–' I cut off when Karim sniggered. 'Shut up.'

'Told you. This is going to be fun to watch.'

'Eat up, Halabi. And be careful not to choke. Smugness and gorging don't go well together.'

'Fun,' he repeated, unperturbed. 'I shall enjoy myself immensely, Mr Three Continents Watson.'

'Three Continents Watson?' Djamal asked, interested.

'Broken hearts in many nations and three separate continents,' Karim said, spearing a chunk of green vegetable. 'Three. Continents. I believe there's a couple of female hearts in your collection as well, am I not right?'

'Quiet,' I said. 'That's all in the past.'

'Didn't seem that way when you were with that fashion victim. What was his name again?'

'Adam.'

'That's right. Adam. Nice enough, but not the right man for you.'

'Oh? And how would you know who the right man might be?'

'Someone with whom you're willing to trade meat for pasta. Oh, wait,' he furrowed his brow, as if in deep thought. 'I believe we have just met a suitable enough candidate. Tall, good hair, great chin.'

'You're an arse.'

'But you love me all the same.'

'I do. Lord have mercy on my soul.'

Djamal looked from me to Karim and back to me, shook his head and laughed.

'I think you and I should go for a drink, John. I believe there's a lot we have to talk about.'

'I should like that a lot, Djamal. There's things I'm sure Karim has failed to mention. Did you know he considered Catholicism at one time because he attended Christmas service with our Irish flanker and thought it was a great spectacle?'

Karim choked on his carrot slice and coughed. I handed him his glass.

'Problem?'

He glared at me over the rim of his glass, and I leaned back, smirking.

'Didn't think so.'

WHEN IT WAS TIME TO PAY, Karim snatched up the bill.

'For keeping you waiting,' he said. 'I'm really sorry about that. And I'm especially sorry for not having had the chance to chat a bit more with Sherlock.'

'Just swing by some time after work,' I suggested. '221B Baker Street. Just text me before you do, so I know.'

'I will,' he promised. 'He seems like a good one. Allah's blessing be upon you.' It was said without his earlier teasing, and I pulled him into a hug.

'Blessings upon you, too,' I whispered into his ear. 'Djamal is a keeper. You chose well.'

'I know,' he whispered back. 'I'm glad you approve.'

I let go of him and clasped Djamal's hands.

'You take good care of him,' I said. 'He is a smug little shit, but I love him like a brother.'

'I've noticed,' Djamal replied. 'I promise I will do my very best.'

'You do that.'

CHAPTER TEN

BEING THE SURGERY'S A&E SPECIALIST DID HAVE ITS MOMENTS, BUT working late on a Friday was not one of them. It was well after eleven o'clock when I finally got home, but when I opened the door to our flat, it was all but yanked out of my hand.

'There you are,' Sherlock said in lieu of a greeting. 'Do you have gay clothes?'

'What?'

'You're a gay man. I'm asking you whether you have articles of clothing that would qualify as gay.'

'Define gay,' I said, put my messenger bag down and shrugged out of my jacket. 'If you're thinking fishnet, glitz, and feathers, the answer is no.'

'You're not the fishnet feathery type. Tight shirt. Arse-hugging jeans.'

I snorted. 'Arse-hugging?'

'Snug,' he said impatiently. 'Tight. Come on, John, you know what I'm talking about.'

'I think I do, yeah. Mind telling me what this is about?'

'I need to go somewhere and it would be better to bring someone.'

'A gay someone?'

'Obviously.'

'Of course. But before we discuss my gay evening outfit, give me a couple of minutes to use the loo, wash my hands and go feed the boys.'

'The boys have already eaten.'

'They have? Thank you.'

'You're welcome. Now hurry.'

I raised my eyebrows at him but before I could say anything he was already on his way into his bedroom. Shaking my head, I bent down to remove my shoes, then went to do what needed doing. It had been a long day, and I was tired, but I knew from experience that if I lay down now, I would stare at the ceiling for hours, too wound up from being on my toes since 6am but too tired to fall asleep. Why not go to a club. With Sherlock.

My wardrobe wasn't exactly an endless source of inspiration, but I eventually pulled out a pair of jeans that had the desired tight fit and a black V-neck tee with a neon print. I hadn't worn either in a while, and, when I had put both on, I studied myself in the mirror, not entirely displeased with what I saw.

'Very buff. Exactly as I had hoped.'

I stared at Sherlock's reflection in the mirror. Faded jeans with rips at the knees and across the thighs and a light blue T-shirt that looked as if it had been splattered with bleach and then been shrunk by mistake. Brown suede brogues and a fedora. And–

'Is that eyeliner?'

'It is. Do you like it?' He came to stand next to me and inspected his work. 'I thought about using liquid eyeliner, but I just can't apply it. I always end up looking like an ancient Egyptian. Kohl is so much easier to use. Do you like it?' he repeated and gave me an expectant look.

'I – uh,' I did like it. A lot, actually. Not sure whether it was the skin-tight clothes or the dark-rimmed eyes that made my mind wander in an entirely inappropriate direction. Both, probably. In any case, not what I needed right now. Not with him standing so close and in my bedroom, too. 'What do you plan to achieve?' I asked, avoiding his question.

'I need to get someone's attention.'

'What, in a gay club?'

'No, at *White's*,' he said. 'Of course in a gay club, John. Do you plan to wear a belt with that?'

'I do, yes.'

'Good.'

He sat down on my bed and watched me get ready. Funny how stubborn a belt can be if your mind is occupied elsewhere. Like telling your hands to not tremble. Or telling your cock to remain at ease.

'Where are we going?'

'Nellie's.'

'Huh?'

'City Road. It's a basement club.'

'What kind of crowd?'

'Gay men, mostly. A couple of women, too.'

'Music?'

'Disco.'

'Disco?' I reached for my boots and bent down to put them on. 'As in Village People?'

'Good heavens, no. As in house and techno.'

'Oh.' When I straightened, I thought I'd caught him checking me out but I wasn't sure. He got off my bed and was out of my room in the blink of an eye.

'Coming?'

I grabbed my wallet and hurried after him. He threw me my jacket that hung by the door, slipped into a blazer and galloped down the stairs. I locked the door to our flat and followed him outside.

NELLIE'S WAS LOCATED UNDERNEATH a nondescript Asian shop. Its entrance was behind a heavy metal door, and I queued up to pay while Sherlock flirted outrageously with one of the bouncers, a heavyset man of medium height sporting an impressive ZZ Top beard. He kept looking over at me, grinning. Just as I was about to pay for our tickets,

Sherlock came, no, *minced* towards me in a way that was decidedly un-Sherlockian, took my hand and pulled me straight to the entrance. No fee for us tonight, apparently. Fine by me.

'You're a lucky man, mate,' the bouncer called after us. 'I would pay good money to eat him out.'

Before I had a chance to figure out which one of us was the lucky man, Sherlock blew him a kiss.

'Sorry about that, Roops, but my Johnny here is the only one eating me out.'

Oh.

Sherlock winked at me and dragged me down a narrow flight of stairs that didn't look particularly trustworthy. I wasn't claustrophobic but I sure hoped this place had an emergency exit. Or two.

Inside, it was the kind of club I hadn't set a foot into since I had broken up with Adam – hammering bass and drums, migraine lights, the usual mix of beards and beauties, bodies writhing around and grinding into each other. A handful of women, too, and two very pretty male dancers on a raised platform in the middle of the dance floor.

Sherlock let go of my hand, pointed at my jacket, made a circling gesture and said something.

'What?'

'I said,' he shouted into my ear, 'drop your jacket, let's do some cruising and then dance.'

I nodded and followed him as he wove his way through the crowd. At the far end of the main dance floor was some sort of cloakroom, guarded by a tall Goth girl with more piercings in her face than I liked to see. Yes, I know, to each their own, but this was just too much metal in one face. I guess I was too much of an A&E doctor to not think of infection and injuries.

I paid for our jackets and pocketed the token she gave me for both.

Sherlock cruised the place as if he was hosting a houseparty in his home, waved at the DJ, exchanged a few words with a very blond barkeeper, received a hug here and hugged back there, all twinkytwunk and pouting very prettily. I found it very hard not to stare at him because, the hell? A heads-up on the way here would have been nice, but after a while I began to enjoy myself and slipped into the muscle role he had apparently assigned to me. I mean, why else the 'very buff' comment? And so I scowled at those who pouted back at him, placed a possessive hand on his nape and when somebody leaned in as if to kiss him, I pulled Sherlock out of the way and against myself, staking my claim for everyone to see. After all, wasn't I the only one eating him out? *I wish.*

'Poor little Andrew here only wants to play,' Sherlock said, melting against my chest. 'You got nothing to worry about, Johnny.'

'I'm not worried,' I replied. 'But he should be.' I gave Andrew, who was anything but little, a stern look and pulled Sherlock closer. 'I'm not the sharing kind.'

Yeah, definitely enjoying myself. It's such fun playing the bad guy.

Sherlock threw his arms around me and nuzzled my neck. 'Let's go dancing,' he suggested and when I nodded, pulled me away, shouting 'sorry' in Andrew's direction.

The day's tension slid off my shoulders as I got into the rhythm and I caught a few appreciative glances from some of the blokes dancing near me. From some of the ladies, too. That was nice, and had I been with anybody else I might have glanced back, but my attention was fixed on Sherlock.

I'd had no idea he could move like that. His lean, angular frame lost all of its sharp edges and became one sinuous curve, swaying and undulating with the hammering beats. There's really no way to dance sexy to that kind of music but he did. He danced in and out of my reach, his eyes never leaving my face, a strange little smile on his lips. He came close enough for our bodies to touch, but only just. No grinding or pressing against me, but this here was infinitely hotter. It was 'look at what I have to offer' and 'all yours for the taking' and 'not now.'

Suddenly he looked up, waved at somebody and mouthed 'be right back' at me. I turned my head, trying to figure out whom he had waved at, but all I saw was three business suits kicking back shots. I tried not to be too disappointed – after all, hadn't he told me he was trying to get somebody's attention? I remembered my role as the muscle by his side, and so I grabbed his arm when he turned to leave.

'Where do you think you're going?'

'Just saying hello to an old friend.' He looked at my hand on his arm. 'Let go of me, Johnny, you're hurting me.'

I doubted that because his arm was all sinew and muscle in my grip but I let go. 'Promise you won't be long.'

'Promise.' He kissed the corner of my mouth and disappeared into the crowd.

I looked after him, then shrugged and raised an eyebrow at the bearded bloke next to me. 'Girls,' I said dismissively and continued dancing as if I didn't care.

Sherlock didn't return for a while, but I wasn't dancing by myself for very long. A very pretty little ginger with the most delightful freckles came shimmying up to me. He looked to be in his early twenties and was wearing a tight button-down shirt with palm trees and the skinniest trousers I'd seen in a long while.

'Hello, handsome,' he shouted. 'Dance with me?'

I gave him a critical stare as if to assess and size up the goods he had to offer. He preened a little, flexed his biceps and raised his chin as if challenging me to decide in his disfavour, but I liked his freckles and his smile and so I nodded and made a gracious *come here* gesture. 'Sure, why not.'

He beamed and soon there wasn't an awful lot of room between us. He danced with as much body contact as humanly possible and judging from the bulge that rubbed and bumped against my thigh, he was interested in more than just dancing. Strangely enough, I wasn't. I liked him and under different circumstances would not have been averse to a little weekend fun – God knows it had been a while – but it was not cute and ginger I was after these days. But his enthusiasm was nevertheless flattering, and so I kept dancing and smiling, let him rub against me, and hoped he didn't notice my lack of interest.

The music changed to a slower beat, and just as I was beginning to worry about having to slow dance with Ginger, an arm snaked around my waist from behind and a tall frame pressed against my back.

'What do you think you're doing, Johnny?' Sherlock said into my ear and bit my neck. Heat shot through me and just like that, I was hard. Ginger's eyes widened as something pressed against him that hadn't been there before, and he understood at once it wasn't he who had caused it.

'Piss off, bitch,' Sherlock hissed. 'This one's mine.'

His arm around my waist tightened and what followed next was the most exquisite form of torture I had ever had to endure. This was not the playful teasing I had undergone earlier on. Oh no. This was the 'let's see how sturdy those fly buttons really are' version.

Damn you, Sherlock.

He pressed himself flush against me, reached for my hand, twined our fingers together and started moving his hips with the slow rhythm of the music. His breath was hot against my skin, and when he kissed the nape of my neck I swear I felt him smile. My whole body tingled, and I wished we were alone, in my bedroom back at 221B, or his bedroom, or the living room, anywhere where it'd be just us, and no clothes. But I wasn't complaining, really. It felt too good, and I didn't want it to stop, didn't want the heat of his body against mine to go away.

When he unglued himself from my back, I felt deprived, but it only lasted a few seconds for he moved around me, squeezing himself between me and Ginger who had not entirely given up hope thus far but who now accepted defeat and backed away, regret all over his features.

Sherlock's eyes searched my face, his gaze dropped to my lips, and he smiled.

I swallowed, held my breath. Would he–

He did. The touch of his lips on mine sent a shockwave through my body, and if this sounds like it's been taken straight from a romance novel, then I don't care because that's what it was. His lips were surprisingly soft as they brushed over mine, as if asking permission. *Oh hell yeah.*

I reached blindly for his hips and pulled him against me, letting him feel that permission had already been given. His eyes widened and so did his smile, then he cupped my face with his hands and deepened the kiss, teasing my lips open with his tongue. I opened willingly, and his tongue glided inside, warm and wet. It made my head swim and the music disappear into the background until it was only the two of us. Sherlock was as hard as I was, and I felt rather than heard him moan when my hands landed on his arse. Turned out his butt cheeks felt just as tight as they looked, and they were a perfect fit for my hands, too.

The beat picked up again, but we didn't care. We swayed to a rhythm only we heard, mouth on mouth, pelvis against pelvis, and cock against cock, one of his hands buried in my hair and the other fisting my shirt, my hands on his arse. I broke the kiss only to lick along the column of his neck, tasting the fine sheen of sweat, which to my lust-crazed mind was fruity-tangy and bubbly-light, like some exquisite, exotic wine. Sherlock tilted his head to the side, granting me better access as I nibbled and licked my way up to the underside of his jaw. He swallowed, and I felt his throat move against my lips.

'Let's go,' he said and reached for my hands.

I nodded and stumbled after him as he pulled me towards the cloakroom. What...oh yes, our jackets. The Goth girl's eyes swept over us and her dark red lips split into a decidedly un-Goth smirk as she took in our state of emergency. She handed us our jackets and called a cheerful 'Have fun, boys' after us as we limped-hurried towards the exit.

The outside air was clear and rather crisp for a June night, but I took a deep breath when we stepped through the door. What a treat after the heat and musky humidity inside, and as we neared the street I turned to Sherlock expectantly.

'Well?'

He let go of my hand without saying a word, fished for his mobile and, hailing an on-coming cab, speed-dialled a number.

'If the sister has just recently dyed her hair chestnut, arrest her,' he said as soon as the call connected. 'And Miranda is go. I'm on my way. Yes, now. Have your bloodhounds ready.'

He rang off and kissed my cheek.

'Bye, John. Take the next cab, yes? I'll see you in the morning.'

Chapter Eleven

I stood and stared as the car pulled away.

What the actual bloody fuck?

I swear I heard my cock wail at being denied what had seemed the natural course of the evening only minutes ago, and by the time the next cab pulled up I had worked myself into a full-on rage.

'221B Baker Street,' I snapped at the cabbie, got in, and pulled the door shut with unnecessary force, which earned me an indignant look and a muttered protest. I apologised half-heartedly and sank back against the worn seat.

'Bye John. See you in the morning, John.'

The fuck was that all about? Heating me up and then leaving? What about his own hard-on? I mean, there was no denying he'd been every bit as horny as I had been. Didn't that bother him? Did he have a magic off-button to deflate his cock when he was done playing?

In fact I was angriest at myself. At no point had Sherlock explicitly indicated he was attracted to me or anyone else for that matter. Yes, there had been looks and smiles but nothing else. Just me hoping. But surely someone not interested at all didn't kiss like he had kissed me, right? There had been enough heat in his kiss to melt the dance-floor. I wouldn't even kiss a potential one-nighter like that.

So what was that all about, good-byeing me like he had?

When we reached Baker Street, my erection had gone, and my rage had simmered down to bitter disappointment. Death by blue balls is an urban myth for teenage boys. Ditching, however, ditching is a thing, and it hurts. No matter how old you are.

I paid the cabbie, added a decent tip for the moment of fright I had given him, and walked up the short flight of stairs that led to 221B.

The moment I switched the light on in the corridor, the squeaking went off. It made me laugh, despite my foul mood, and after taking my boots off I walked up to the cage where Bodie and Doyle sat by their wooden house, looking up at me expectantly.

'Who needs motion detectors when there are guinea pigs,' I said. 'Hello, lads. I guess you want a midnight snack, yes?'

Squeak.

'Thought so. Be right back.'

I went into the kitchen, turned on the light and inspected the mess on the small table and the worktop. Plates, cutlery, pots, a coffee cup and a glass. And the people section of today's, no, yesterday's newspaper. So Sherlock had not only eaten but had actually taken the time to sit down to eat. *Good.* I considered it a personal victory when I found he'd actually eaten the food I had put into the fridge.

I put the dishes into the dishwasher and rinsed the pots, muttering to myself about the ungratefulness of certain flatmates, about making assumptions and my own stupidity, about still cleaning up after him after all he had done, and, when I was done muttering and cleaning up, I chose a red pepper as a midnight snack for the boys, quartered and sliced it and walked back to throw the pieces into the food bowl.

'Your uncle Sherlock is an arsehole,' I told them. 'Can you believe it, he fired me up all the way and then left me standing there all by myself.' No reaction but the sound of rapid chewing. 'Of course you don't care. You're all set, the two of you.'

On the way to the bathroom I moved my armchair back where it belonged and picked up a shirt and one lonely sock, threw both into the laundry basket along with my clothes and took a quick shower. I briefly considered an equally quick wank, but, after giving my cock an experimental tug, I decided against it. We were both too disappointed and so I towelled myself off, brushed my teeth, and padded into my bedroom where I slipped into my bed, naked and alone.

Pissing Sherlock.

SHERLOCK DIDN'T SHOW UP the next day, but I didn't think much about it. He occasionally stayed at Mycroft's, and I assumed that's where he had gone. I spent the morning cleaning up, doing laundry, going grocery shopping, the usual. In the afternoon I headed off for the Royal London Hospital for my volunteer work and got home around 7pm on Sunday. Sherlock still wasn't there, and, given the fact our flat was as neat as I'd left it the day before, he hadn't been home at all.

I frowned and checked the answering machine. Nothing. He hadn't texted me, either. Now that was unusual. He usually left a sticky note by the phone or sent a short text. I called up Mycroft's number on my mobile, stared at it but after a moment of thought decided against ringing him. If he was anything like Sherlock claimed he was, then he was a worse mother hen than I was and would most likely create a fuss I didn't want to get caught in.

I forced myself to sit down on the couch and flicked through the TV channels. The usual inane mixture of soap operas, reality shows, quiz shows, and a selection of super-cop shows with actors who looked so alike that I couldn't figure out which show I was watching.

I eventually stuck with a news channel. Suicide bombings and gunfights, hundreds of civilians dead, military strike considered a success despite regrettable collateral damage. A female serial killer arrested in her East London home. Seven people arrested and charged for drug trafficking and money laundering after early morning raids at Peckham and Harlesden addresses. On to the weather.

When the doorbell rang, I woke with a start, heart hammering in my chest. Our doorbell didn't actually ring. It went off with as much charm as an alarm clock, only 15 times louder, and it had just moved up by five notches on my list of things to replace.

Another ring, longer this time.

'Bloody hell,' I shouted and got up from the couch. 'Forgot your key or what?'

I pressed the door opener and heard the main door click open. There was a grunt and a *thud*, and an unknown voice called up to me.

'Dr Watson? Dr John Watson?'

'Yes?'

'I need a hand here.'

'What is it?'

'It's Holmes.'

The hell? I slipped into my trainers, grabbed my keys, and ran downstairs. A tall woman in a brown suit stood by the door, panting heavily, trying to support Sherlock, whose left arm she had slung around her shoulders.

I rushed to help her and the moment I took Sherlock's right arm, he stirred to life.

'John, 's you,' he slurred, freed himself of the woman's hold, and slumped against me. 'I 'm home, yeah?'

'You're home, Sherlock,' I confirmed, struggling to hold him upright. 'All good now. Can you walk?'

Sherlock mumbled something unintelligible into my chest. Without further ado I freed myself from his grip, looked him up and down, and, when I had convinced myself he wasn't suffering from extensive injuries, hoisted him up and over my shoulder, like a sack of grain. He groaned something and giggled, and I braced myself for the long journey up the 17 steps that led to our flat. My leg protested vehemently but cooperated well enough.

I carried Sherlock into our living room where I gently lowered him into his armchair.

'Sherlock, can you hear me?' I asked, crouching down before him.

'Mhm,' came a sleepy reply. 'John?'

'Yes, it's me. It's all good now, I'm here.' I reached up to switch his reading lamp on. 'Open your eyes for me, please?'

He blinked and flinched when the lamplight hit his eyes. Both his pupils constricted. I shaded him from the light, and his pupils dilated. *Good.* His right cheekbone was bruised but the bone structure seemed intact. His lower lip was split and swollen.

Behind me, someone coughed politely. I had forgotten all about the stranger for a moment, and, with a barely suppressed groan, I got up from my crouch.

The woman nodded towards Sherlock. 'Will you need help with him?'

'I don't think so, thank you. Can you tell me what's happened?'

She visibly struggled with herself.

'He was, uh, caught in the middle of a situation,' she finally said.

'So I figured, given his bruises and the cuts,' I replied sharply. 'I bet there'll be more once I remove his clothes. What kind of situation?'

She reached into her pocket and produced a card, which she handed to me. 'Why don't we speak tomorrow. Here's where you'll find me. My mobile number's on the back.'

The card said: *Detective Inspector Gwendolyn Lestrade.* It also said: *New Scotland Yard.*

Wait, what?

'You're with the police?' I asked, incredulous. 'Has he done anything wrong?'

'Quite the contrary,' Lestrade replied with a thin-lipped smile. 'He's done everything right, and then some.'

'I'm sorry but I don't follow.'

'You don't have to. Come and see me tomorrow and if possible, bring him with you. I will need his statement.'

She turned to leave.

'Wait,' I said. 'Why didn't you take him to hospital?'

She shrugged. 'He refused to step into an ambulance, saying the only doctor who's allowed to touch him was a certain John Watson. We had quite a situation on our hands, and the paramedics had more urgent cases to tend to, so I had him take the backseat of my car. As soon as circumstances allowed, I came straight here.'

'I see. Well, in that case, thank you very much, Inspector.' I held out my hand and we shook. Her handshake was firm but her hand was cold and a little clammy. I didn't hold that against her, though, because she looked dead tired. 'I'll look after him, and if he's well enough tomorrow, I'll make sure he comes to see you."

'Thank you, Dr Watson. And good night.'

I accompanied her to the door, thanked her again, and watched her make her way downstairs. When the main door had fallen shut behind her, I locked the door to our flat, toed off my trainers and went back into the living room where Sherlock was struggling to get out of the armchair.

'Whoa, what do you think you're doing?' I grabbed him by his arm to steady him. 'Won't you let me examine you first?'

'Shower,' he slurred. 'I reek.'

'Yes, you do.'

He did, too. Quite horribly so. What on earth had he been doing? And drinking? He was still in his club outfit, but his fedora was gone and his kohl was smeared, making him look like a cross between a panda bear and Alice Cooper.

'Wait,' I said when he started fumbling with his trouser buttons. 'Shoes first.'

I knelt down to unlace his brogues and removed them, then pulled off his socks. He bent forward and held on to my shoulders. When I straightened, he straightened with me, still holding on to me.

'Thank you, John,' he said slowly, making an effort to speak more clearly.

'What for?'

'Being here.'

'I live here,' I reminded him.

'Not that.'

I gave a non-committal grunt and gave his face a searching look. He stank of alcohol but did not seem under the influence of drugs. He looked exhausted and battered, in urgent need of a shower and some sleep.

'Let's get you into the bathroom,' I suggested. 'Will you be able to take a shower by yourself?'

'Dunno. Mebbe.'

Probably not. I slung his left arm around my neck, much like the inspector had done earlier, supported his waist with my right, and half dragged, half pushed him into the bathroom.

Here, I helped him out of his clothes. It wasn't quite the scenario I had envisaged not too long ago, but, firstly, I don't take advantage of someone obviously not within his full mental capacity, and, secondly, the instant his shirt came off and I saw the bruises that adorned his upper body, I switched to full doctor mode, which meant my sex drive turned off at once.

'Good God, Sherlock, what happened to you?'

He didn't answer. He didn't have to. Sherlock looked as if he'd been clubbed to death. Well, almost. He was with me, thankfully, and not lying on some stretcher in that morgue he liked to visit. Other than that, he looked awful. There were bruises on his chest, his arms, his back, all shades of red turning purple and blue. He was soon going to look like one of those blue-skinned guys from *Avatar*, and I didn't think I had enough lotion at home to treat all of the bruises.

I peeled his trousers and underpants off. His legs didn't look quite as bad, and luckily the long scar had not suffered further damage. His right knee was badly scraped and a little swollen – nothing an ice pack couldn't heal, I hoped – and his left shin was going to sport a bruise to match the ones on his upper body. And still, it seemed he'd been lucky despite all, for there were no bleeding wounds, except for a few superficial cuts. A quick exam showed no suspicious sensitivity in the abdominal region. No teeth missing, either.

'Do you think you can take that shower by yourself?' I repeated my earlier question. 'Or do you want me to help you?'

He scowled at me, as if insulted by the suggestion, but he swayed when he tried to climb into the bathtub and his shoulders slumped.

'Will you help me? Please?' His voice held a mixture of resignation and annoyance.

'Of course I will.'

I pulled my shirt over my head and my socks off my feet but kept my jeans on, if only to signal Sherlock he didn't have anything to fear from me. He did not appear nervous at all when I climbed into the bathtub with him but leaned against me, fully trusting and without so much as a hint of bashfulness as I soaped and rinsed his bruised body as gently as I could. I washed his hair, too, remembering the amount of hair product he had used.

'Eye make-up remover,' he mumbled and swatted my hands away from his face when I tried to wash off the smeared kohl. 'Don't rub the shit into my eyes, John.'

'Where is it?'

'Above the sink. Cabinet.'

'All right. Let's get you dry and out of the tub. Then you can take care of your panda make-up.'

He managed a weak chuckle. 'Not so sexy anymore, huh.'

'Not at all,' I confirmed, switched the water off and climbed out of the tub, careful not to let go of Sherlock's hand. He was a bit steadier now than he had been before but better safe than sorry. When I had him safely out of the bathtub, I towelled him off and wrapped the towel around his hips.

While he fumbled for his eye make-up remover, I got my own towel and, glancing over my shoulder to check what he was doing, quickly pulled down my wet jeans and briefs and wrapped the towel around my hips.

'All done,' Sherlock finally announced. 'One shouldn't remove eye make-up with regular soap, John. Not good for the eyes. You use face wash or pads like these.' He held up a box.

'Thank you for letting me know. I shall keep it in mind the next time you come home looking like you've been hit by a double-decker.'

He gave me a crooked grin and winced when his split lip protested. 'Guess I'm in no position to smart-arse right now, eh.'

'As long as you smart-arse about, you're not seriously hurt. Will you let me treat some of the worst bruises before you go to bed?'

'Yes, please.'

'Good lad,' I said approvingly. 'Don't move. I'll be right back.'

'I need to piss. I will have to move for that.'

'Yeah, well, do what you need to do and call me when you're done, 'kay?'

'Yes, John.'

I closed the door behind me and went into my bedroom for a pair of dry boxers, then fetched the arnica lotion, an ice pack for the knee, and some ibuprofen and went to get a glass of water, switching the living room's light off on the way back.

I waited for the toilet to flush, then knocked on the bathroom door.

'Yes, come,' Sherlock shouted and I walked in.

'Here's something for your pain,' I said, handing him the ibuprofen and the water. 'Two should do the trick.'

He wrinkled his nose. 'I don't do painkillers. You know that.'

'Doctor's orders,' I replied. 'You're not going to test drive the Batmobile tonight so shut up and do as I say. You need some rest, and you won't get any once your body catches up with what's happened and starts hurting. Come on, don't be ridiculous.'

He frowned and eyed the ibuprofen as if I was handing him a live scorpion to swallow but gave in after a brief staring contest and swallowed two pills.

'Good lad,' I said again. 'Now let me get some arnica on your prettiest bruises.'

He stood stock-still while I applied lotion to the most prominent bruises, but by the time I was done he was shivering.

'Are you all right, Sherlock?' I asked, searching his face.

He had turned white as a sheet but nodded stubbornly. 'Everything is fine. Don't worry about me.'

His pupils were dilated, and he was blinking rapidly. I reached for one of his hands. Freezing cold.

'Off to bed now. At once.'

'I'm fine, John.'

'No, you're not.'

I took his bathrobe from its hook by the door, pulled the wet towel away from his hips – why hadn't he put his robe on after he'd used the toilet? – and wrapped him into the reddish monstrosity.

'You are not fine, Sherlock,' I repeated, sternly, 'and you will go to bed at once.'

He didn't reply, just looked at me out of eyes that were suddenly huge and frightened, and nodded. I took him by the arm and led him out of the bathroom.

'Can you get into your – no, you can't. Tell you what. You'll sleep in my bed tonight, and I'll take the couch. No way I'm letting you climb up that ladder with you shivering like that.'

I steered him into my bedroom, pulled the blanket back, and helped him lie down, then secured the ice pack with a bandage. He let it all happen without uttering a word of protest, and I must say, that did worry me a little. It was a very un-Sherlockian thing to do, obey without protest.

I tucked him in and checked his forehead for signs of a fever. Nope, all good.

'Well then, I'll leave the door open so I'll hear you. If you don't feel well or if anything starts hurting, just shout, okay? I'll be right over there, on the sofa, and I will come when you call. Yes?'

He nodded, but when I switched the bedside lamp off and turned to leave, he reached for my hand.

'Don't leave, John. Please. Stay with me. Please.'

I looked down. There was nothing playful or flirtatious in his face, nothing that would indicate he intended to continue whatever game he had played Friday night. He was pale and he was shivering, a delayed shock reaction finally catching up with him.

Climbing into bed with a patient was highly unprofessional, but this wasn't a hospital, and he wasn't my patient. I lived here and he was my flatmate. Who was feeling miserable. Right? Right.

And so I nodded. The instant I stretched out next to him, he inched closer so our bodies almost touched.

'Thank you,' he whispered.

I stared straight ahead into the near-darkness of my bedroom, then looked at him. He had his eyes closed, and the shivering had subsided a little, but it was still there. *What the hell.* I stretched out my arm, wrapped it around Sherlock's shoulders, and pulled him against me.

And there we were. In my bed. Half naked. Just as I had wanted.

Only – not at all as I had wished for.

CHAPTER TWELVE

I WOKE UP THE NEXT MORNING TO SOMETHING TICKLING MY NOSE. I BLINKED from sleep into consciousness, slowly, slowly, and froze when realisation hit me. It was Sherlock's hair that tickled my nose because Sherlock was in my bed, lying on his side with his legs pulled up a little – and I was glued against his back like a perfect big spoon, complete with my arm around his waist and my morning wood snug against his butt.

I carefully loosened my grip and tried to bring some distance between us as gently as possible but Sherlock stirred, made a sleepy, content sound and snuggled closer against my chest. Against my boner, too.

'Morning, John.' His voice was thick with sleep but he sounded like himself again. Certainly more than he had last night.

'Morning,' I replied. 'Sleep well?'

'Mhm.' He turned around so he came to lie on his back. 'I did, yes.'

'How are you feeling?'

He frowned and his gaze turned inwards. Probably running an internal system check.

'Fine,' he finally said.

'Fine? Really?'

'Allow me to rephrase to satisfy your medical curiosity. I believe I'm fully functioning, and no major systems have come to serious harm. I feel as fine as one would after being caught in the middle of a

– uh, a situation, but I have slept surprisingly well and feel sufficiently recharged to face and survive the chore of answering DI Lestrade's questions.' He took a deep breath. 'Better?'

'Much better,' I approved. 'How would you feel about some breakfast?'

He made a face. 'I'm not sure I feel that fine.'

'Hey. Are you saying my breakfast is not good?'

'Oh, it usually is but I'm not a breakfast person. You should know that by now.' His stomach gave a loud rumble.

'Of course you aren't,' I said and sat up. 'Let me throw something together and you decide then, yes?'

'Okay.'

I rolled out of bed. 'Mind if I use the bathroom first, or do you really, really have to go?'

'Go ahead. My bladder will hold.'

'That's good to hear.'

He snorted and turned to lie on his side again. I grabbed a pair of jeans, a shirt, and a fresh pair of boxer briefs, padded into the bathroom and groaned when I took in the chaos. It looked exactly as we had left it the night before. Of course it did. Unlike Sherlock's lordly brother, we did not have a household staff at our disposal to clean up our mess.

Before I went into the kitchen to make breakfast, I rang the practice. It was 7.45 already, and, although I was certain I had no patients scheduled before eleven, I needed to let the team know I was probably going to be late. Sherlock had sounded as if he could make it to the police station to file his statement on his own, but it wouldn't hurt to be on standby, just in case.

I fed the boys first and then set up the breakfast table for the humans, opened a box of Sherlock's favoured cereal (very colourful, zero nutritional value) and started the coffee maker, got the kettle going, poured some juice. Whatever the invalid felt like partaking of.

'Sherlock?'

No response. I went into my bedroom and nearly laughed out loud at the sight that greeted me. Sherlock had crawled into the middle of the bed, blanket pulled up under his chin and his nose buried into…my pillow. My laughter stopped mid-throat. It may sound cheesy but I will not deny that my heart beat a little faster when I saw him hug the damn thing to his chest like that.

'Adorable' is not a word you want to use when describing a grown man, nor will a grown man ever be caught using a word exclusively reserved for puppies unless he's talking about actual puppies, but Sherlock did look adorable. His hair stood up in mad tufts, his sharp features were relaxed, and the corners of his mouth curved slightly upwards, as if he was smiling at something only he could see.

Of all the things I found attractive in Sherlock it was his smile that had my stomach do a little flip and made my knees go wobbly each time it appeared. When Sherlock smiled – a real smile, not one of those non-committal, conversational half-smiles and not a smirk either – his eyes lit up, his face softened and a little dimple appeared by the left corner of his mouth, and I had caught myself more than once or twice wondering whether I'd kiss his lips first or that dimple and nibble my way along his jawline, either towards his stubborn chin or towards that sensitive spot behind the earlobe…

In all honesty, I had liked waking up with him in my arms, and I had liked it even better when he had stirred and cuddled into my arms, all sleep-heavy and pliant. What I wouldn't give to be able to crawl underneath the blanket with him and kiss him a very good morning.

Not happening now. Not before he had healed some more, not before I knew what exactly had happened to him the night before…and certainly not before he had told me what on earth he had been thinking, leaving me behind the way he had. I now felt sure he wasn't indifferent towards me, not after clinging to me like he had after Lestrade had hauled him home and certainly not after crawling into my bedding the way he was doing right now, before my very eyes.

But this was not the time to wonder whether or not to cross a bridge that had not yet come into view. Only, it had. To some extent. I had already set one foot on it and remembered what it had felt like.

Get your shit together.

And so I resisted temptation, placed my hand on Sherlock's shoulder and gently shook him.

'Hey, sleepyhead, wake up.'

He half groaned, half yawned and cracked one eye open.

'It's alive,' I said with mock surprise. 'Good morning, dear. Breakfast is served.'

'Mhm.' He pulled the blanket up to his nose. 'Don't wanna.'

'Oh, but you do.' I pulled the blanket down and away. 'And I don't have all morning. Your bruises need checking and you will eat before you see the inspector.'

He swatted at my hand but it was a half-hearted attempt, and, after another yawn and a joint-cracking stretch, he rolled out of bed, drew his bathrobe around himself, and shuffled into the bathroom with the pained expression of one dragged out of bed in the middle of the night. I shook my head, folded the blanket back and smoothed the pillows, lingering longer than necessary in the attempt of catching the echo of Sherlock's body warmth with my hands.

When he joined me for breakfast a while later, he was wearing a pair of navy blue trousers and a pair of brown Oxfords, with a white shirt hanging unbuttoned from his shoulders.

'What's this? Got a bank appointment or what?' I asked, looking him up and down with raised eyebrows.

'Worse,' he said and handed me the arnica lotion. 'I'm meeting Mycroft for lunch at his club.' He shrugged out of the shirt and hung it neatly over the back of the chair. 'I put that stuff to the worst bruises but I can't reach all of them on my back. Will you help me with that?'

'Sure.'

He turned around and I winced when I looked at his back. Yes, I was a doctor, and, yes, I'd seen worse, but seeing a wounded stranger is different from seeing a wounded friend. He stood perfectly still as I applied the lotion and only gave a short hiss when I rubbed across a particularly nasty one.

'Sorry,' I said. 'What was that about meeting Mycroft at his club? Are you telling me he's actually a member of one of those gentlemen's clubs?'

'He is,' Sherlock confirmed. 'But don't ever call it a "gentlemen's club" like that to his face or he will hurt you.'

'With what? Flick one of his business cards into my face?'

That made him laugh. 'Never underestimate the impact of a properly flicked business card.'

'I quiver with fear.'

'My brother's not the pencil-pusher people take him for. His mind is like a scalpel. The sharpest you'll ever come across.'

I looked up at the barely concealed note of brotherly pride in his voice. 'Are you telling me your brother is a double agent in Her Majesty's service?'

'Don't be absurd. He's too fat for that.'

'Don't let him hear that, or you'll be the one who ends up with a business card in his face.'

'Wouldn't be the first time.'

'Oh?' I capped the tube and went over to the sink to wash my hands. 'Bully big brother?'

'Insufferable little brother, more likely,' Sherlock admitted with a small grin and sat down.

'Like that, eh. Tea or coffee?'

'Coffee, please. Can't face Lestrade and Mycroft in one morning without your witches' brew.'

'The club must be a rather distinguished place if you dress up like that.'

'Oh, it is. *For Christ's sake, Sherlock, it's where gentlemen meet,*' he said in perfect imitation of Mycroft's clipped speech. *'Put some effort into it.'*

I laughed and sat down after pouring each of us a cup of coffee.

We ate in silence which was unusual because we tended to chat comfortably when we sat down to eat together. Sherlock wasn't much of a breakfast person, true, but when he did join me in the mornings he often chatted about whatever occupied his mind: an article on toxicological and histopathological studies he had brooded over the night before; the reverse pentatonic scale and its effects on albino mice; Bodie's potential involvement in a fascinating experiment...

(*'Absolutely out of the question.'* *'But John, think of the data he'll provide!'* *'No, Sherlock, and it's not a no that's up for discussion.'*)

...and society and celebrity gossip. He studied the tabloids as if they held new insights into the holy script, and, to be honest, I found his discourses on entomology easier to follow than the endless stream of names I had never heard of.

Nothing of that kind today. I chewed through my toast and eggs while he ate his cereal. How did you not talk about the fact that your flatmate had been escorted home by Scotland Yard? How did you avoid asking for the cause of the horrible beating he'd taken? How did you un-bluntly ask what the fuck he'd been thinking getting you all horny and wanting and then wandering off to receive said beating? (Although I was fairly certain he had not planned for the beating to happen.)

And then there was one more thing that needed clarifying.

'Listen, Sherlock, I'm sorry,' I said into the strained silence.

He looked up from his bowl. 'For what?'

'I – uh,' I cleared my throat and set my knife and fork down. 'I'm sorry for crawling into you the way I did. That must have been awkward.'

'Crawling into me?' He frowned.

'In bed,' I said. 'While we were sleeping, I mean. I was all over you. I'm sorry about that.'

'Oh, that.' He ducked his head, pushed a red loop away from the green ones. 'I actually liked it,' he mumbled into his bowl.

'What?'

'I said,' he repeated and met my stunned gaze with a small smile, 'I liked it. It felt…good.'

'Really?'

'Mhm.' He busied himself with his sugarloops again, but I swear his cheeks had turned a little pink.

'So,' I said in a conversational tone, 'mind telling me what–'

My mobile rang. Great timing. I considered letting it ring but I'd just told the surgery to get in touch and although I couldn't think of anything that urgent at 8.30, we were a surgery with a small A&E department. Which had exactly one doctor on its staffing list. And so I got up to fetch the phone.

Not the practice.

'Morning, Karim,' I said. 'Is that a new habit of yours, calling in in the wee hours of the morning?'

'It's eight-fucking-thirty,' he replied. 'Why the hell aren't you at your operating table, transplanting livers and saving lives?'

'Because Sherlock got caught in a situation and needed my help.'

'Situation, eh? Some enraged client not happy with the results he delivered?'

'No idea. So, what do you want?'

'My late afternoon meeting got cancelled and I thought it's about time I dropped by. I mean it's been a month or so since we've met for dinner. Ramadan is nearly over. Are you free tonight?'

'I am, yes. Not sure about Sherlock.'

'Shame. I can't stay for very long anyway. My sister has invited Djamal and me for tonight's *iftar*.'

'You better not be late then or Lina will serve your head to break the fast.'

'With three dates on the side.'

'Probably. Sure, drop by as soon as you get off work. I should be home around six or seven.'

'Long day?'

'I have three surgeries scheduled this afternoon. And a staff meeting.'

'And the staff meeting is the one that really hurts.'

'Probably. So, see you tonight?'

'Tonight. Now go and tend to your patient, Dr Watson, and then save some lives.'

'Will do.'

'*Yalla salaam*.'

I put my phone down and turned around.

'Sorry–' I began but Sherlock wasn't there. He reappeared as I was cleaning up, now fully dressed in a smart business suit minus the tie, the very image of dapper if not for the bruised cheekbone and split lip. I commented on that but he made a dismissive gesture.

'I'll tell Mycroft you beat me,' he said.

'Please don't. Death by business card is not what I want to see on my death certificate.'

'We'll falsify the records. Shall we? You're coming with me, aren't you?'

'If you want me to, then yes, I will. But I don't think it'll be necessary. You look stable enough to take on bureaucracy by yourself.'

'Not necessary, no. But there's something I need to take care of, and I will need you for that.'

'Do I want to know?'

'Not right now you don't.'

CHAPTER THIRTEEN

I HAD NEVER SET FOOT INTO NEW SCOTLAND YARD AND WAS NOT AT ALL prepared for what greeted me. I had known about the Met moving into another building – it had been all over the newspapers – but I had not given it much thought, thinking it would be just another governmental monstrosity once you got past the flashy façade.

Well, it wasn't, and I felt a little overwhelmed as I followed Sherlock into the entrance pavilion with its curved glass walls.

'Yes, pretty,' he said after he had given our names to the front desk officer who picked up his phone immediately. 'All new and shiny. Still has the same old policefolks in it, sadly. This way.'

He led the way with long strides, and I hurried to keep up with him. Was he allowed to just walk wherever he liked?

Seemed he was, and we reached the lifts unhindered. Sherlock pressed a button, and we rode up to the fourth floor where Lestrade already stood waiting.

The DI looked considerably more alive than she had last night, and, when she shook my hand, hers was no longer cold nor clammy. The dark rings under her eyes weren't as pronounced anymore, either. She was a tall, wiry woman who looked to be in her mid-40s, with chin-length brown hair, the barest touch of make-up and hazel eyes that held an intent, alert look.

'Good morning, Dr Watson,' she greeted me. 'Holmes.'

She gestured for us to follow her. We walked through an open-space area that looked nothing like I had imagined a police station to look like. Officers sat perched on stools at some kind of bar while others sat in groups on sofas arranged to form impromptu meeting zones. I was reminded of how investment analysts sat huddled together, or at least how films portrayed them. Much like what Karim described his workplace to be.

'Yes, the Met has arrived in the 21st century,' Lestrade said when she noticed my surprise. 'Time will tell if it was a smart move.'

We followed her into a niche where a desk and two visitors' chairs stood.

'Before we get started,' Sherlock said as he sat down, 'the reason I brought John along is that I'd like you to list him as my emergency contact.'

'Whatever for?' I asked. Wasn't Sherlock here to give some kind of statement about last night's events? I had wondered why he had insisted I come with him but had shrugged it off as one of his ideas. Was there more to it?

Sherlock leaned back in his chair and crossed his legs.

'Inspector?'

Lestrade nodded after a moment. 'Go ahead.'

'I consult for the Met,' Sherlock explained. 'The reason Lestrade, uh, escorted me home last night was that I got caught in the middle of a situation that got slightly out of hand, and, as it was part of an on-going investigation, she considered it her duty to deliver me personally into your hands.'

'The hell you're saying?'

'I'm saying that I work for the Metropolitan Police, John, on a call-by-call basis.'

So that was the secret behind Sherlock's irregular comings and goings. It also explained the nature of the official-looking files I sometimes found him brooding over. I hadn't been all that wrong with my assumptions then, but I hadn't expected his work to be on that scale.

I looked at Lestrade. 'Is that true?'

'Of course it is true!' Sherlock sounded indignant. 'I already told you when we had dinner with your friends. Did you think I was making this up?'

'No, I didn't. It's just unusual, isn't it? I had no idea the police worked with civilians.'

'We do occasionally,' confirmed Lestrade. 'Although it's more commonly done in the more technical lines of police work, extremely specialised forensics or high level IT cases, for instance.

'Holmes has been very helpful for a very long time, uncredited and unpaid, and after some extensive paperwork and even more kowtowing we were finally able to offer him a consultancy agreement.'

'Which I eventually signed, after some perusal and a few changes.' Sherlock added and Lestrade grimaced. 'Come, Lestrade, it wasn't that bad, was it?'

'Not at all, Holmes. Just got me a few more grey hairs.'

'I know the feeling,' I said. 'So, copper consultant, eh? No offence, Inspector.'

'None taken.'

'Consulting detective,' Sherlock corrected me. 'That's what it says on the agreement.'

Sherlock nodded to Lestrade. 'Well? Is that going to be a problem?'

'Not at all. Let me pull up the necessary forms.'

'While you're at it, I want him to be granted full access to all necessary information in case of me not being of sound mind and disposing memory. Temporarily or otherwise.'

Lestrade looked up from the keyboard.

'Are you sure?'

'Of course I am. John?'

'Uhm, if that's what you want?' I didn't like the sound of that. At all.

'It is,' Sherlock confirmed with a firm nod.

'What about your brother?' Lestrade asked.

'He's family. Of course he's to be contacted. But from now on, I want John to be my primary contact. You know what Mycroft's like.'

They exchanged a look, then Lestrade nodded but said with a frown, 'That'll take some more paperwork.'

'Well, have it prepared, then,' Sherlock said impatiently. 'Can it be sent to us for John to sign, or does he have to come in?'

'I'm afraid it'll have to be signed here in person. You will need to bring a valid ID with you, Doctor.'

'That's all right.' I took out my wallet and got one of my cards. 'Here's where you can reach me during practice hours, and this,' I scribbled my mobile number on the back of the card and handed it to her, 'this is my private number. If anything like last night happens again, ring me. If anything else happens, ring me. Please.'

'Understood,' Lestrade said and, giving me a sharp look, placed my card on her desk between keyboard and screen.

'So,' I said, folding my hands in my lap, 'now that I've officially been made Sherlock's primary contact, mind telling me what happened last night? No sensitive details, of course, just a rough sketch so I understand what I'll be dealing with in future.'

Careful what you wish for.

What followed was something taken straight out of one of those extremely popular and utterly nonsensical television shows – drug trafficking and money laundering under the very noses of London's law-abiding citizens, and, to add some more spice to this near-indigestible dish, an apparently sociopathic female on a killing spree to rid this city of male 20-somethings with three stars tattooed on their forearms. It all sounded vaguely familiar, and when Lestrade mentioned Peckham and Harlesden, I remembered.

'Wait,' I said. 'Wasn't that on the news last night?'

Lestrade nodded, and I rubbed my hands across my face, visions of explosions and back-alley shoot-outs ghosting through my mind.

'Does that happen a lot?'

'Choosing a doctor as a flatmate was a smart move, is all.'

'Funny, Sherlock. Clown for breakfast, yeah?'

CHAPTER FOURTEEN

HAMMERING BEATS GREETED ME WHEN I RETURNED FROM MY USUAL Saturday round of gym and grocery shopping. I dropped my bags and went straight into the living room to turn the volume down, then checked on the guinea pigs. Their cage was covered with a wool blanket, and when I lifted it, two sets of eyes peeked at me from their little house door where they sat huddled together. Loud noise did not agree with them.

'Poor boys,' I said. 'I take it you don't approve of Uncle Sherlock's work soundtrack?' I grabbed a handful of hay from the bag that sat next to the cage. 'There you go. Sorry about that.'

I looked around and suddenly remembered what Tony had told me when the possibility of a flat-share first came up. Was that what he had meant when he had said Sherlock was 'a little eccentric?' It sure looked like I had moved in with a mad professor.

The television was set to what looked like an Asian news station, and three laptops sat on the coffee table, two of which were running a search with a program I'd only ever seen in TV shows, and the third one was opened to a well-known gossip site. Whatever the latest fling of some minor Hollywood starlet would have to do with the fancy search programs or – I took a closer look at the telly – the Tokyo stock exchange, I had no idea.

The mass of paper spread out in a neat circle in the middle of the room made even less sense. There were newspaper clippings, some shreds of paper that appeared to have been ripped out of a magazine and a few police reports that surely weren't meant to be openly spread out in some bloke's living room. A half empty mug sat dangerously close to the edge of the table, and I moved it to safety, eyeing the tar-black contents with disgust.

Where was said bloke anyway? The bathroom door stood wide open and the amount of humidity wafting through the door told me Sherlock had finished one of his steam-bath shower sessions not too long ago.

I picked my grocery bags up from where I had dropped them, put them on the kitchen table for now, and went over to the chicken ladder that led up to Sherlock's bedroom.

'Sherlock?' I called. 'You there?'

'Up here,' came Sherlock's voice, sounding as if he was farther away than just his bedroom.

I frowned. 'Up where?'

'Come and see.'

With a sigh I climbed up the stairs. Sherlock was not in his room.

'Are you hiding in the closet?'

'Outside.'

Outside? Surely he didn't mean – but the roof-light stood open. He did mean it. I looked outside and there he was, stretched out on the roof tiles, lying on his shirt as if it was a towel, the legs of his trousers rolled up, letting the early summer sun warm his naked skin. The sight of his bruises still made me wince inside, but they were beginning to fade. He was…well, gorgeous. I swallowed and for a quick, crazy moment wondered what his skin would taste like. It wasn't hot enough outside for him to sweat (and for another and even crazier moment, a vision of how that could be changed danced through my brain), but his skin probably felt warm from the sun. No hair on his upper body but for a thin trail wandering from his navel down to disappear into the waistline of his jeans.

'Come on up, John,' he said lazily and cracked one eye open. 'It's nice up here.' The expression on my face made him laugh and he sat up. 'It is not dangerous and unless you're all dressed in silk and satin you will not slip off.'

'I know that,' I replied indignantly, tested the window-frame for stability and hoisted myself up and through the window.

Sherlock moved over and I cautiously sat down next to him.

'Look at this,' he pointed, 'Regent's Park. Pretty, isn't it? I find it very relaxing, having something green to look at in the middle of the city.'

'So that's why you needed access to the roof? To have something pretty to look at?'

He shot me a side glance. 'No,' he slowly said, 'I don't need to climb on the roof if I want pretty. Although, pretty is not the word I'd use in this context.' He reached over to the side and held up a packet of cigarettes. 'I didn't think you'd want me to smoke in the flat.'

'You thought right. I had no idea you smoked.'

'Doesn't speak for your observational skills.'

'Do you expect me to sniff you when you come home?'

'Would you like to?'

'You haven't eaten,' I said, not taking the bait. 'You haven't eaten at all yesterday and you haven't touched breakfast this morning. Please don't tell me you're on a diet.'

'Don't be absurd. I'm working.'

'And?'

'I don't eat when I work.'

'Why?'

'Eating slows me down.'

'Why?'

'You get sluggish after a meal, with all of your blood rushing to your stomach to digest what you've just stuffed yourself with. I need to stay sharp and alert.'

'And so you don't eat at all?'

'No. I do drink, however.'

'Yes, I saw the brew on the table. What on earth is it?'

'It's called Raising Hel, and it's a Finnish coffee brand. That's 'Hel' as in Nordic underworld, not 'hell' as in devil.'

'Smells pretty horrible.'

'Ah, but you should try it once.'

'Thanks, but no thanks. And you think this is healthy, to not eat but live on Finnish superbrew?'

'I'm still alive, am I not?'

'It would seem so. But you don't have to starve yourself if you have some thinking to do.'

'It's all a matter of self-discipline.'

'An exercise in abstinence?'

'I am not a monk. I work with my head. I think. I observe. I analyse. It all happens in here.' He tapped a finger against his temple. 'My body serves the brain. An appendix, if you want. Once the brain is at work, all else fades into the background. I require no food, no rest, no sleep until I'm done. Work always comes first.'

'That has got to be the biggest pile of shite I've heard in a long while.' It came out harsher than I had intended and Sherlock stiffened.

'My dear John—'

I raised a finger, stopping him in mid-sentence. 'Don't you my dear John me, my dear Sherlock. I get your point of not stuffing yourself when facing an intellectual challenge. I do, really. A bout of gluttony is not recommended in my line of work, either; in fact, gluttony is never recommended. Neither is sleeping yourself into a stupor. But denying your body the basics it needs to function? Not good, Sherlock, not good at all. Depriving your body of food can lead to blood sugar imbalances, and that can well lead to headaches, sweating, trembling, and fatigue. I don't see how any of these side effects will help you get your job done.'

'But—'

'If you want to think well,' I continued, ignoring him, 'you've got to eat well. And not only every once in a while. I'm sorry, Sherlock, but you chose a doctor to be your flatmate, and, as a doctor, I can't listen to such nonsense and not tell you what I think about it. Do yourself a favour and have some breakfast at least. A bowl of porridge–'

He made a face and I laughed. 'All right, no porridge. Some cereal, a slice of toast, a handful of fruit and nuts, a yoghurt. I promise you will not feel stuffed and your brain will thank you for it. And your body.'

'Do you think that's necessary?'

'I do, yes. Will you not give it a try? For a couple of days, until your thinky thoughts are thunk?'

That made him grin, if a little reluctantly. 'All right, Dr Watson, I surrender to your doctor's wrath. Breakfast it is. But I can't guarantee I won't forget.'

'I'll prepare your food for you. All you have to do is eat it.'

'You like to do that, eh.'

'What, look after a stubborn git? Not particularly.'

He smiled and my heart did a little flip in my chest. *Careful, John.*

'You're a mother hen, John.'

'I've heard that before. The stubborn git in you brings out my protective instinct, I guess. Can't blame a man for wanting to look after his...flock.' *Family. Loved ones.* But that was taking it a bit too far, wasn't it? I hoped he hadn't noticed my near stumble.

If he had, he didn't show it. 'Very well. Breakfast it is.'

'Good lad,' I approved. 'It'd be a shame to let that appendix go to waste. If you did, you wouldn't be able to maintain your running routine. And you'd soon be too weak to swing that Kendo stick of yours.'

He didn't disagree with that and said as much. Then, 'It would be a shame, huh.'

'It would indeed.'

'You really think so?'

'I do, yes. It's a very nice appendix your brain has there.'

'Thank you.'

We fell silent and I looked about and at the rooftops of London. Or rather, of Baker Street. It wasn't the most picturesque corner of London but it wasn't bad, either. And if I shifted around just so, Regent's Park came into focus and it really was relaxing, all that green. And it was nice in the sun, too. I closed my eyes.

'I'm a good runner but I wish I had more upper body strength.'

'Mhm?'

'What you just did? Getting onto the roof like that? I couldn't do it. I have to push-pull myself and do some climbing.'

'That's what I did, too.'

'But it looked easier.'

'That's because I eat.'

He huffed. 'Got the message.'

'Good.'

'And, John?'

'Yes?'

'Apologies for leaving you behind the way I did. At *Nellie's*, I mean. That wasn't a kind thing to do.'

'No, it wasn't.'

'But I needed to be somewhere.'

'I get it. Work always comes first.'

'Thank you for understanding.'

'You're welcome.'

CHAPTER FIFTEEN

'Will you take a look at this, John?'

'Mhm?' I looked up from the newspaper. 'Take a look at what?'

Sherlock was sitting cross-legged in the middle of the living room, a number of photos arranged in a neat half-circle around him. Some of them showed the upper half of a woman's body. A dead woman's body, as far as I could tell from where I sat. He pointed at two of them.

'These two photos. There's something I cannot figure out.'

'Is that another pub quiz or are you seriously asking for my opinion?'

'Neither. I'm asking for your input as a man of medicine.'

'Oh.'

I put the newspaper down and walked over to him. 'Which ones?'

'These here.' He pointed and I bent down to look.

'May I?' I reached for them but hesitated mid-move.

'They're photos, not evidence. You will not contaminate a crime scene if you pick them up.'

I grunted in reply and looked at the photos. One was a close-up of the dead woman's face, the other included her torso. She looked to have been in her mid to late 40s, hair tied back and showing a hint of greying roots, one eye was made up, the other wasn't. She was wearing a baby blue turtleneck that was smeared with blood and she seemed to be lying on a bathroom floor, blood pooling out from underneath her.

'Looks like she was stabbed,' I offered.

Sherlock snorted. 'Thanks for that.'

'Well, what do you expect from me? It's two photos of a dead woman, not her actual body.'

With a deep sigh, Sherlock stood up. 'She was stabbed four times,' he said, pointing. 'The knife slid off her ribs twice, here, but the other two stabs were fatal. One to the abdomen, one below her left breast, here and here.'

'Oh God.'

I looked at her face. She'd been a handsome woman – strong features with a straight nose and a generous mouth and blue eyes that now stared unseeingly into nowhere.

'What happened?' I asked. 'I mean, was it a break-and-enter kind of thing and she just happened to be there? Or was it cold-blooded murder?'

He shrugged. 'The police believe it was breaking and entering because the jewellery is missing, as is the IT equipment and the stereo and TV. I don't think so. It all has a rather staged feel to it.'

'How do you mean?'

'It very much looked like you'd expect it to look. Drawers open, underwear half in, half out, cushions everywhere, chairs upside down. Would you bother with the dining room chairs if you were looking for valuables?'

'Probably not.'

'See.'

'Who found her?'

'Her husband.'

'Oh God,' I said again. 'Poor fellow.'

'Don't poor fellow him too much.'

'Why is that?'

'I'm convinced he's lying.'

'Alibi?'

'Pub after a rock concert with friends.'

'His friends vouch for him? And were they sober enough to be taken seriously?'

'Most of them were, yes. He received a call from his wife just after their first round, rushed home and found her dead. His mates say he was very upset after the call, saying his flat was broken into, his wife was scared, and he had to go at once. One of them insisted he even heard the wife cry for help.'

'What's that red spot underneath her chin?' I asked, pointing at something that had me puzzled.

'I have no idea,' Sherlock said. 'That's where I was hoping your medical expertise would come in.'

I looked at him sharply, but there was no sign of mockery in his face, and so I took a closer look.

'It's no bruise and it certainly is no livor mortis,' I said. 'I've seen something like that before but where?' I looked at the close-up some more, looked up and stared at a spot on the opposite wall, trying to remember. I squinted. Was that—

'Please tell me you haven't been throwing darts at the wall with the target removed,' I groaned.

'I was bored and you weren't here,' he said, a little defensively.

'Why, would you have thrown the darts at me instead?'

'Of course not. Don't be ridiculous, John.'

'So it was my fault exactly why?'

'I needed someone to talk.'

'What did you want to talk about?'

'Just…things.'

'Things.'

'I wanted to follow a train of thought.'

'Ah,' I said. 'I see. You mean you wanted to talk at me, not to me.'

'Where's the difference?'

'Following a train of thought usually implies you performing a monologue instead of engaging in a proper conversation, you know, as in bouncing thoughts back and forth.'

He huffed. 'Semantics.'

'No, Sherlock. Monologue means only you talk. Conversation means you and I take turns talking. Anyway, please put the target up next time unless you want Mrs Hudson to have a coronary.'

And then it hit me. Out of the blue I remembered where I had seen a similar red spot before. Just – what would Sherlock have to say about that?

'What is it?' he asked. 'You look like you're about to have a coronary yourself.'

'Your concern is touching. I think I have an explanation for the red spot.'

'Let's hear it.'

'This,' I tapped my finger against the photo, 'this looks like a burn mark.'

He frowned. 'Nonsense. That's no–' He stopped when I held up my hand.

'Hear me out,' I said. 'It's obviously not a burn mark as in having been subjected to an open flame. Some two or three years ago I treated an elderly lady with marks that looked just like this one. I first thought she'd developed some kind of food or fabric allergy but why did the marks only ever occur on the very same spots and nowhere else on her body?'

I made a dramatic pause but as Sherlock did not seem too excited to hear about my patient I continued before he'd turn his attention elsewhere. 'Turned out she'd taken to napping wrapped up in her electric blanket and the thing didn't turn off as it was supposed to do, causing these mild burn marks.'

'I don't see what this – oh. Oh!' His eyes lit up. 'That's it! That's brilliant!' He grabbed my face and kissed me smack on the lips. 'Why didn't I think of that?' Another kiss, this one to my forehead. 'Thank you, John.'

He took the photos from me, stepped back into the half-circle of crime scene photos, dropped to his knees, and reached for his mobile that sat on the file to speed-dial a number, gathering the photos together while he waited for the call to connect.

'Lestrade, the Tinnings case,' he said without preamble. 'Have the M.E. take another look at the red mark underneath the wife's chin. – Yes, the one that looks like a bruise but isn't. – I don't care what the technician said, have the M.E. look at it again. – I know the body's about to be released. Think of something. – I don't know. Make something up. Then, set up an interview with the husband. And his mate, uh, Norden. Get a search warrant, too. We're looking for an electric blanket or something similar. – Yes, electric blanket. Something your grandmother might use. – Because I think the body was wrapped in one to keep the temperature up. – Why?'

He looked at me, then looked up at the ceiling and closed his eyes. 'To make it look as if the time of death has occurred later than it actually did. Get it?'

He scrambled to his feet with considerably less elegance than before. Being exasperated seemed to rob him of his coordination, it would seem.

'I'll see you in 30 minutes. I need to talk to you,' he gave me a sideways look and winked, 'about the red flannel shirt, too. Yes, 30 minutes.'

He rang off, then looked at me. 'Hope you haven't anything planned for the night that involves me. I don't know when I'll be home.'

'Oh, never mind me. It'll be nice to catch up on *Lewis* without you telling me who did it and why.'

He was already on the way into his bedroom and I doubted he had heard me. But when he came back down a couple of minutes later, dressed in his version of smart casual which included his indispensable Dr. Martens, he said, on his way to the door, 'You're only watching that boring show for Sergeant Hathaway and don't you try to deny it.'

I put down my newspaper. 'Say what?'

'Dishy Hathaway,' he repeated. 'Tall and a bit haughty, yes?'

'Shut up. Don't you have a murderer to convict or something?'

'Hathaway,' he said, pronouncing each syllable, and shut the door behind him before I could say anything else.

He was right, of course. Although I did not find the show boring, I did watch it mainly because of Hathaway who, yes, was tall and bit haughty. Great voice, too.

MY MOBILE RANG JUST as I was about to start the DVD.

'What now,' I muttered when I saw the name *Holmes* appear on the screen, but when I picked the phone up I realised it was not *Holmes, S* but *Holmes, M.*

'Hello,' I said, surprised.

What could Mycroft possibly want from me at – I checked my watch – 7pm on a Thursday? Rather: what could Mycroft possibly want from me at all? We'd never spoken since his first and only visit to Baker Street.

'Good evening, Dr Watson.'

'Good evening, Mr Holmes.'

'Have I caught you at a bad time?'

'Not at all.'

'I find myself with a free evening on my hands and I wondered whether you'd like to join me for dinner.'

What? *Wrong Holmes to ask me out on a date.*

'Sure,' I cautiously said. 'Is everything all right, Mr Holmes?'

'Why do you think otherwise?'

'You've never called me before.'

'I see. You're worried about my motivation.'

'Not particularly worried. Surprised, maybe.'

He gave a low – and unexpectedly attractive – laugh. 'I assure you there's no hidden agenda, Dr Watson. It is as you said – we've never spoken, despite the fact that you've been living with my brother for almost three months now.'

'Funny how time flies.'

'Indeed. What do you say? If you have other plans I'll understand. It was just an idea.'

'No other plans,' I said, giving Sergeant Hathaway one last look before switching the DVD off. *Some other time, handsome.* 'Where would you like to meet, and when?'

'How about the *Isoletta*?'

Never heard of it before. 'What's that?'

'It's an Italian restaurant on Northumberland Avenue. Near Whitehall Gardens,' he added.

I could take the Bakerloo line then and get off at Charing Cross or maybe Embankment.

'Got it,' I said. 'Italian sounds good. Is there a dress code?' I couldn't imagine Mycroft Holmes supping at your average come-as-you-are restaurant.

'There is,' he replied. 'Smart casual. No jeans, please.'

'Understood.' I bet this Holmes' idea of smart casual differed from the other Holmes' interpretation. 'What time?'

'Would 7.45 be too soon? Or 8pm?'

'7.45 is all right. I'll take the tube.'

'I'll make a reservation for 7.45. See you in a bit, Dr Watson.'

'Later,' I said and rang off.

What was that all about? Why did Mycroft suddenly feel the need to get to know me? Had anything happened? Sherlock hadn't – he certainly hadn't said I'd beaten him up? Or had he, and Mycroft had taken it seriously?

Sherlock had a way of saying things that sometimes ended up all wrong. But surely his brother...*Bollocks*. No way he'd ask me to join him for dinner if he thought I was abusing his baby brother.

I Googled the *Isoletta* and gulped. Smart casual indeed. It looked as if it was part of a posh hotel. As in, very posh. After a good hard moment of deep consideration, I opted for a combination of good, classical colours with clean, classical lines. Adam, my ex, had not only liked clubbing, he'd loved shopping, and while he hadn't turned me into the fashion-savvy beast he was, I'd still picked up a thing or two.

It was 7.25. Better get going.

CHAPTER SIXTEEN

WHEN I ARRIVED AT THE *ISOLETTA* I WAS LED TO A TABLE IN A CORNER OF the restaurant that was quiet enough to allow for some privacy but offered a good overall view as well. Mycroft was already seated, scrolling through his messages on his mobile but rose to greet me. I looked at his impeccable navy pinstripe three-piece suit and congratulated myself on choosing smart over casual.

'Mr Holmes,' I greeted him.

'Please call me Mycroft. Thank you for making time at such short notice, Dr Watson.'

'John, please. Nothing to thank me for. I had nothing in particular planned.'

We sat down, and a waiter appeared out of nowhere. The menu was impressively short, and I settled on the marinated bluefin tuna as a starter and the grilled beef tenderloin as my main course. If I was to have dinner in a restaurant like this one, might as well do it right. Then I studied the wine list, frowning. I liked wine well enough, but, to be honest, I didn't know an awful lot about it.

'Will you please choose the wine?' I asked Mycroft, putting the wine list down. 'I'm afraid I'm out of my depth here.'

Seemed Mycroft appreciated my honesty, for he nodded without so much as a hint of contempt at my admitted ignorance, and, after asking if I'd already decided what to eat, engaged in a lively conversation with the waiter. In Italian.

'That's settled then,' he said in a satisfied tone when the waiter had disappeared. 'Ernesto just loves a good debate before accepting one's choice.'

'You didn't seem to mind so much,' I remarked and he laughed. It was the same throaty laugh that had sounded so attractive over the phone, and it was even more attractive in person.

Wait, what?

It sure said a lot about my current state of mind if I was beginning to find a suit like Mycroft Holmes attractive.

'True,' he admitted. 'It's all part of the game, isn't it.'

'What is? Haggling?'

'Yes. Don't you agree?'

'No,' I said. 'I don't. I prefer to say exactly what I want and how I want it. Makes things easier. Beating around the bush is just such a waste of time.'

He looked at me. 'I see.'

Before I had a chance to ask what he meant, a waiter – not Ernesto but a much younger bloke – arrived with a bottle of water. Then the chef himself made an appearance, greeted Mycroft like a life-long friend, greeted me, too, in much the same fashion, and presented us with an *amuse bouche*, hinting at the delicacies to come with all the bubbly excitement only an Italian chef can muster.

I hoped that we weren't going to be attacked every other minute and said as much as soon as the exalted chef had left.

Mycroft smiled. 'I should hope not. The open fire usually ceases once Samuele has presented the *amuse bouche*. I must warn you, however, he will return when we are done.'

He reached for the water and poured us each a glass. 'How are you, John? How is life with my little brother?'

I pointed to my temples. 'See that? I'm going grey. And fast, too.'

He toasted me. 'I wish I could say *told you so* but, alas, I wasn't privy to your decision. Is it really that bad?'

'No,' I said and eyed the *amuse bouche*. 'What's that supposed to be?'

Mycroft inspected the tiny bite that was tastefully arranged in a nest of what looked like carrot and cucumber spirals sitting on a plate I would have chosen for a healthy serving of penne.

'It appears to be aubergine and feta,' he ventured.

'Aubergine, huh.' I picked the thing up by the delicate pick it was speared on and sniffed. 'I think you're right.'

He was. Aubergine and feta. Not bad, actually.

'So, Mycroft, why did you ring me up? Why the sudden interest?'

He shrugged. 'Nothing sudden about it. I had lunch with Sherlock on Monday, and he mentioned you, uh, nursing him back into consciousness. It was there and then that I thought I should like to get to know you a little better.'

I circled the rim of my glass with my index finger. 'You realise this sounds a little off, yes? Are you trying to find out whether or not my intentions are honourable?'

He visibly started. 'Lord, no. I'm truly sorry if I come across like that.'

Ernesto appeared with our starters. My tuna looked fantastic and so did Mycroft's mozzarella. Amazing what you can do with a pale cheese and some tomatoes. We focussed on our food, grateful for the chance to reconsider the somewhat awkward turn our conversation had taken.

'What I really wanted to tell you in person,' Mycroft said after a while of concentrated chewing, 'is that Sherlock looks happier and healthier than he has in a long while. I'm fairly certain that's mainly your doing, so…thank you, John. All this detective work he's been doing may be good for his intellect, but he's got a regretful tendency to push all else aside when there's a case to be worked on.'

'Don't I know it.'

'Yes, I think you do. But he tells me, among other things, that you cook for him and you force him to eat, too–'

'Hey,' I protested, 'don't make it sound like I'm tube-feeding him. And I'm not cooking just for him. I need to eat, too.'

'So you urge him to join you for your meals,' he corrected himself with a faint smile, 'and what's more, he obviously listens to you. He's lost that haggard look that's been greatly worrying me.' He speared some mozzarella and tomato and chewed, a thoughtful look on his face. 'He told me he's taken up composing again.'

'Composing? As in, writing music?'

Mycroft nodded.

'Wow,' I said, impressed. 'I had no idea. He plays a lot, especially when he's brooding over something, but I had no idea he actually writes music.'

'There was a time when he seriously considered becoming a professional violinist.'

'Why didn't he?'

'Chemistry was more interesting.'

'Ah. Experiments and all.'

'Exactly so. Tell me, John, have there been, well, let's call them appearances of items that do not belong in the place they appeared?'

'Like eyeballs in our freezer?'

Mycroft closed his eyes with a pained expression. 'He didn't.'

'Oh, but he did.'

I told him about the eyeballs marinated in guinea pig food and the crickets and the mealworms and how I had come home one evening to find something unspeakable dribbling off the kitchen table onto one of the chairs, with Doyle sitting in my casserole, safely out of reach of whatever was dribbling, and munching on a huge chunk of watermelon.

'Who is Doyle?'

'One of my guinea pigs.'

He frowned. 'Guinea pigs? Oh yes, I remember seeing a cage in a corner.' He cast me an amused glance. 'Aren't you a bit old for guinea pigs?'

'You're never too old for guinea pigs,' I said. 'But if you must know, I got them from my nieces.'

'Has Sherlock experimented on them yet?'

'They are off limits, and he gave me his word.'

'And you believe him? Why else would he place – Doyle, yes? – into a casserole?'

'I told him I'd bust both his kneecaps if he harmed the boys.' It was out before I could help myself, and I quickly continued. 'He likes having an audience when he conducts his experiments, to share his findings. Makes him appear less of a mad professor muttering to himself, I guess. And while a guinea pig is a living, breathing audience, it won't contradict his deductions.'

Mycroft didn't take offence at me threatening his little brother with physical harm. Instead, he chuckled and provided me with a few anecdotes about experiments young Sherlock had conducted in their parents' house. Some of them made me bite back bouts of laughter, some of them made me shudder, hoping he'd never find it necessary to repeat them.

By the time our main courses were delivered, we were on easy chatting terms, and I found out Mycroft was not as uber-protective of his little brother as I had feared, and when we touched upon the subject of me having replaced him as Sherlock's primary emergency contact at the police, it turned out he not only knew but approved of it, too.

'It does make sense,' he said, neatly cutting into his salmon fillet. 'I'm a hard person to get hold of, and when I'm stuck in negotiations, which regrettably is the case more often than not, I make it a point to mute my mobile phone.'

'What is it you actually do?' I asked.

'I work for the government,' Mycroft said.

My eyebrows shot up. 'Really?'

'Office work, mostly. I'm not sure what Sherlock has told you, but I am certain he exaggerated. I'm not part of the double-oh programme, in case you were wondering.' He grinned when he saw my face. 'So he's still spreading the rumour, eh.'

I shrugged one shoulder. 'It sounded exciting.'

For the rest of our dinner, the conversation revolved mainly around economy and sports. Mycroft was a fascinating person to talk to. There was hardly a subject he couldn't touch upon, and, as the evening progressed, I found myself wondering more and more what kind of an 'office worker' he really was.

'Thanks for a very enjoyable evening, Mycroft,' I said when we parted. 'We should do this again some time.'

'We should?' He looked genuinely surprised.

'Sure, why not? I had a good time. Didn't you?'

'Did I – yes, I guess one could say so. Good night, John.'

'Night, Mycroft.'

Only when I sat in the train on the way home did it occur to me that while I'd freely shared my personal details with Mycroft, he'd given me almost nothing in return. Now that I thought about it, I didn't know much more about him now than I had before dinner. Office worker, huh. Expert interrogator, more likely.

Sherlock was going through one of his warm-up routines on the violin, and Bodie and Doyle were playing catch on the carpet when I got home. He didn't greet me, something I'd grown used to and didn't take personally. I had learnt by now that playing his scales and etudes helped him 'defrag his mind,' as he called it.

'I had dinner with your brother,' I said into a pause.

'What?' He lowered bow and violin and turned around to look at me.

'That's pretty much how I felt when he rang me up, but I actually had fun.'

'You had...fun,' he repeated. 'With Mycroft.'

'I did, yes. Your brother is an interesting character.'

'Whatever did you talk about?'

'Oh, he showed me photos of you as a child.'

'He did not!'

The horror in his voice made me laugh out loud.

'Don't worry, he didn't. He merely wanted to get to know his brother's flatmate.'

'So he interrogated you,' he said, his eyebrows raised. 'That's your idea of fun?'

'Don't be an arse, Sherlock.' I bent down and grabbed Bodie, who gave a shrill squeal of protest. 'Sorry, mate, cuddle time.' I sat down in my armchair, placing Bodie on my thigh. 'Don't widdle on me,' I warned him and started scratching his back. 'How did it go with Lestrade?'

'Tinnings confessed. In his own living room. We didn't even have to haul him to the station.'

'Oh yeah?'

'Yes. He stabbed his wife before he left for the concert, rang his friend in a fit of panic, friend suggests wrapping the body in the electric blanket to keep the body temperature up, they're off to the concert, friend rushes to the Tinnings' house after the show, rings Tinnings from wife's mobile, rushes to the pub, and arrives just in time to ask Tinnings why he's already leaving, pretending he was there all along.'

'Wow,' I said, impressed. 'Nice job, Sherlock. Congratulations.'

'You were the one to bring up the electric blanket. I hadn't thought of that. So thanks, John.'

'You're welcome. Did he say why he did it?'

'Constant verbal abuse. Upper class woman marrying middle class man and determined to remind him of it for the rest of his miserable life.'

I made a face. 'Lovely.'

'Yep.' Sherlock raised the bow and tucked the violin back under his chin. 'What do you want me to play?'

'What, is it make a wish time?'

'Well?'

'How about you play that intro from *Lord of the Rings?*'

'So predictable,' Sherlock murmured, but I heard him anyway.

'You offered.'

'What is it with hobbits? They're neither tall nor haughty.'

'They have good songs, and they like their ale.'

He raised his eyebrows and shook his head, but he played the piece and he played it well, as always. Bodie seemed to like it, too. By the time Sherlock lifted the bow from the strings, my little friend had stretched out on my leg. Which was treacherously damp. *Little shit.*

CHAPTER SEVENTEEN

'WHAT TOOK YOU SO LONG? ISN'T WEDNESDAY USUALLY A SHORT DAY? I was waiting for you to get home.'

'I had a pint with Karim. Why did you wait for me?'

I dropped my bag and followed Sherlock into the living room.

Was that my old army shirt he was wearing? It was. And it looked good on him, too.

'I want to practise pushing hands with you.'

'Practise what?'

'Pushing hands,' he repeated. 'It's another form of t'ai chi in which a partner is required. Take off your shoes.'

I raised my eyebrows but did as I was bid. 'What now?'

'Come here. Stand right in front of me. No, like this, here,' he grabbed my wrist and pulled me at arm's length before him. 'Yes, like that. Now move your hand towards me as if you wanted to push me away.'

He demonstrated and I mirrored his movements.

'Not so quickly.'

I slowed down.

'Yes, that's it. T'ai chi is all about going with the flow. This is not a combat session. Go.'

I pushed and he met my palm with his, moved along with me and out of the way, gliding to the side with the incoming push.

'Pushing hands is about teaching the body to resist meeting force with force, but to redirect it and yield to it,' he said and moved with my next slow motion push. 'You train your senses to feel your partner's intention. His strength, too.'

I looked at him sharply. Was there something he wanted to tell me? But he wasn't in analysing mode. His voice was soft, and he didn't fire his words at me the way he did when he was doing his deducing thing.

'Again,' he said and I pushed. We repeated this a few times, then he told me to change the angle and blocked my push with the back of his hand, slid his hand along my forearm, and came to stand behind me. 'Again.'

I slowly got the hang of it and, the moment I found a stable stance and understood how to move my hips and shoulders as one ('your right shoulder and right hip are one solid column'), he began pushing me, and I was the one to yield. It was something I'd not done before. I was used to observe and attack, not accept and yield, but after giving in to the slow, fluid motions I began to enjoy myself. It was a little like dancing under water, I thought, one took the lead and the other followed. Only, it wasn't exactly following. It was more like, accept the lead and redirect.

It was also strangely intimate, moving in such synchronicity, anticipating the other's moves and yielding to them, and making the moves and being met. Sherlock's eyes never left my face, and soon he was smiling that little smile he had smiled back at the club. My world narrowed down to our bubble in which we moved with and around each other, and, although the only touching points were hands, arms, and shoulders, it felt as if his body was an extension of mine, or mine of his. It was extraordinary, and I felt a pang of regret when we got to the closing posture.

For a moment we stood there, well within each other's personal space, close enough that I could feel his body heat. Our slow motion dance was over, but the connection between our bodies was still there.

What now?

My gaze dropped to Sherlock's lips that were slightly parted. I smiled. He smiled back.

His mobile went off.

'That's Mycroft,' he said with regret in his voice. 'I'm sorry but I have to take this.'

The moment was over. *Shit.*

He snatched up his phone and disappeared into his bedroom. Déjà vu. Left behind just as things promised to get interesting. At least I didn't sport a boner, so it wasn't as painful as the last time. Still disappointing, though.

I went into the kitchen to fetch me a bottle of beer and checked to see if the boys had eaten. They had and their bowl was still a third full. It made me grin. Let Sherlock mock the fat rats all he wanted, but he fussed over them as much as I did, if not more. So he chose to push his physical needs aside and mine, too, but he sure didn't ignore theirs. Where did that put me on his priority list?

With a sigh I opened the bottle, went back into the living room, sat down on the couch, and reached for the remote control. There was nothing on the telly, the newspaper lay in various crumpled heaps I didn't feel like sorting through, and the book I was reading was in my bedroom. And so I decided to go to bed, at not even half nine. But before I climbed between the sheets, I treated myself to a long shower. And a good, thorough wank.

THE SOFT CLICK OF MY bedroom door being opened yanked me from the brink of sleep back into consciousness, and I turned to squint at the intruder.

Sherlock stood in the doorway, his silhouette outlined against the soft light filtering in from the living room. I couldn't make out his features.

'Sherlock? What is it?'

He didn't reply, remained in the door as if he was hesitant about something. I propped myself up on an elbow.

'Everything okay?' I asked, alarmed.

He moved across the room as quickly and quietly as a shadow, sat down on the edge of the mattress and placed a finger on my lips.

'Shhh, John,' he whispered, pulled the blanket away and slid in next to me.

What the...? I moved over to make room for him, wondering whether he was in the mood for nightly snuggling, whether he didn't want to sleep alone, or whether – well, whatever else was going on in that complex brain of his. I simply didn't want to try and figure out his motives. Not now.

But, despite the daydreams I'd been harbouring ever since our night out, I wasn't prepared for him to press his mouth on mine, wasn't prepared for his tongue to probe my lips nor his hand to slide under my shirt. I automatically reached for him to draw him against me and found him rock hard and that, I wasn't prepared for at all. I pulled back, surprised.

'Sherlock–'

He cut me off with another kiss, and, the moment our tongues touched, I was past caring. He kissed me like he had back at *Nellie's*, deep and intense, and he felt beautifully solid in my arms, much better than my daydreams, all smooth skin and sinewy muscle, his hard cock rubbing against mine. There was a brief flash of disappointment when he swatted my hand away, not allowing me to reach for either his cock or his arse, but then he pushed me on my back and straddled my thighs, intensifying the sensation, and all disappointment was forgotten. I could have continued kissing and rutting, and happily so, but he pulled away, breaking the kiss and a desperate near-whine escaped me.

Not again. Not now. *Please, Sherlock.*

'Your shirt, John,' he murmured and reached for the hem. 'It has to come off.'

I lifted my arms, and he pushed the shirt up and over my head, flung it carelessly aside. His hands roamed my torso, spread across my chest, and he made an appreciative sound, as if he'd just proven a theory right, then rubbed his thumbs over my nipples, slowly, slowly, and lightly flicked against them. I sucked in my breath. My nipples usually weren't all that sensitive, but with him? Wherever his hands went, wherever he kissed and nibbled, my skin tingled in response.

With his mouth and his fingertips he traced the trail of hair leading the way down to the waistband of my boxers. I fisted the sheets and squeezed my eyes shut, hoping.

'The pants really must go, too.'

It was whispered right next to my belly button, and my cock hardened some more. Now there was a sensitive spot all right, and I nodded wordlessly, not trusting myself to not beg.

Please, please, oh God yes, please.

He got off my thighs and with one swift movement pulled my boxers down. They landed on the floor, his pyjama bottoms followed, and he straddled me again. His balls brushed against mine, and it was like an electric jolt through my entire system. He gave a soft hiss, and I saw his cock twitch. A single glistening drop formed at the tip.

He leaned forward and licked along my throat.

'I like your throat. It's strong and sexy,' Sherlock murmured. 'Everything about you is strong and sexy.'

He bit the side of my neck. Not hard enough to leave a mark but enough to make me gasp and buck up. I wanted – wanted so much. Everything. All of it. All of him. I was ready to bury myself deep within him, but if he wanted to do the fucking, I would gladly open my legs for him. Just...please.

'Where do you keep lube and condoms?' he asked against my skin.

'Cabinet,' I managed. 'Drawer.'

He leaned forward and stretched to open the drawer, fished for the desired items. I let my hands travel across his shoulders and down his back, feeling his muscles shift with his movements. He was lanky, yes, but he sure wasn't bony. I had known all along, had seen him stripped down to his underwear and out of it, too, but it was one thing seeing him and quite another to finally be able to touch. That one time when I had held him under the shower didn't count. He'd been my patient back then, trusting me to help him, and my memories were that of a badly bruised body. Hardly fantasy material, and it was time to replace those memories with something more inspiring.

I licked across that sensitive place where neck meets shoulder and felt him shudder. Thus encouraged, I reached for his arse and squeezed. He stilled above me but didn't move out of the way. His arse was a fine fit for my hands, his buttocks taut and rounded, just as I remembered and exactly how I liked. I spread his cheeks and slid a finger between them, wanting to test him, find out just where he intended to take this. Feel his reaction, hear him utter a sound of agreement or protest. Do some deducing of my own. Investigate…

My fingers slid into something slippery, slid further down and encountered…a slicked hole.

Sherlock had prepared himself before coming to me.

Chapter Eighteen

My cock went from ready and willing to fully alert and primed for action. I dug my fingers into Sherlock's buttocks and ground up and against him with a moan.

'Don't,' he gasped. 'Wait.'

He squirmed out of my reach and tore one of the small plastic packets open with his teeth. I reached for the condom, but he shook his head.

'No. Let me.'

His long, sinewy fingers closed around me, as if to gauge the level of hardness, and he gave a small experimental tug.

'So sexy,' he said again, and I pushed into his hand with a needy sound.

'God, your hands, Sherlock,' I choked out, hardly recognising my own voice. 'I've wanted your hands on my cock since the first time I watched you play your damn violin.'

He gave a low chuckle, sheathed me in latex without much ado and clicked the lube bottle open to squirt a generous amount of gel into his palm, brought both palms together, and blew into the hollow to warm the gel up a little.

I lay there, passive, and watched. I didn't dare touch him – I guess I was afraid that despite all we'd already done, the kissing and the rutting...if I reached for him now he'd vanish, and I'd wake up horny and alone. But his hands slicking me up felt real enough.

'Are you ready?' he asked, got on his knees, and spread his legs over my hips.

Was I ever. I nodded, aligned my prick with one hand and guided him with the other. When the head of my cock pushed past the ring of muscle, Sherlock drew a hissing breath, and I dug my head back and into my pillow. It was intense, so tight and so hot, like tiny flames licking along my prick and up to my navel, and I gripped the sheets, moaning through clenched teeth as if in pain. Which wasn't all that far away from the truth. I sure was hard enough to hurt.

Sherlock stopped half way. 'Does that feel good?'

'Oh hell yes.'

I pushed myself up into a half-sitting position and Sherlock immediately leaned forward to claim my mouth, cupped my face with his hands, and forced my lips open with his thrusting tongue. I placed my hands high on his legs where hips and thighs were joined and brushed my thumbs across the sensitive skin on the inside. Sherlock gasped into my mouth and sank down all the way.

Neither of us moved for the next few breaths. We both needed a moment of utter stillness – Sherlock, because his body had to adjust to the intrusion because, yes, it always feels like an intrusion at first, no matter how much you want it; I, because the urge to thrust upward into that tight, hot hole threatened to overwhelm me. I tried breathing through my nose on the inhale and through my mouth on the exhale in an attempt to keep myself under control and not spoil the moment. The sight of Sherlock straightening again and lifting himself up until only the tip my cock was buried inside him did not help, and, when he came down again in one swift glide, I clutched the sheets and cried out his name. Followed by a healthy, heartfelt curse that made him laugh.

Then he started to move, and the thinking part of my brain shut down. The soft light coming in from the living room took away his sharp angles, making him look – well, not exactly otherworldly but certainly a lot more ethereal than I knew him to be, a slender, almost fey creature riding me in a slow, unhurried way. He took my breath away. Shadows and light danced across his upper body, throwing a merciful shroud over most of his still prominent bruises, his eyes were closed, and his head was tilted slightly backward. His cock bobbed against his stomach with each move, and I made a choked sound, aching to touch.

Sherlock brought his head forward and opened his eyes.

'Put your hands on me, John,' he said in a husky voice.

I hurried to oblige.

'Harder,' he commanded, and I tightened my grip.

'That's it.' Sherlock reached behind to steady himself on my thighs, and I pulled my legs up a little for support.

'You're so fucking tight,' I choked out and drew a sharp breath when his hands curled around my legs in an iron grip. I tightened my hold on his length some more, and he gasped.

'I heard you in the shower, John.' He pushed himself up and into my fist. 'The door wasn't closed all the way, and I could tell by the irregular splashes what you were doing. I heard the sound of your fist on your cock.'

It should have mortified me, and, at any other time, it probably would have, but right now? The idea that he had listened and identified the sounds coming from the bathroom for what they were was enough of a turn-on to make my cock harden some more inside of him. He must have felt it, too, because he tilted his pelvis to adjust the angle and, when he had found the position he needed, gave a low, guttural groan; a beautiful, utterly filthy sound. I loved it.

'I imagined you pleasuring yourself, and it got me so hard.' He rocked his hips with considerably more urgency than before. 'I so wanted to join you. Would you have liked that? Me joining you in the shower?' He groaned again. 'Tell me, John, would you have liked that?'

'Yes,' I managed from behind clenched teeth.

'Next time.' He ran his hands across his chest and down towards where I still had him in a tight grip. His fingers closed over mine. 'I'll join you and suck you off next time.'

'I would like that a lot.'

'Thought so. But I wasn't sure I'd be welcome, and so I stayed outside and listened. I tossed off to the sounds of you tossing off, John. And I came like a rocket. In my bloody pants. Imagine that.'

Imagine that.

And there went my self-control. My hips jerked up, and Sherlock met me on the downward slide with equal force. My shout mixed with his and my bedroom filled with our groans and gasps and the unmistakable scent of sex mixed with sweat, rich and musky. It was impossible to say just who was fucking whom. I might have been the penetrative and Sherlock the receiving partner, but he took his pleasure exactly how he wanted it and dominated me with each rocking of his hips and each downward thrust, and I thoroughly lost myself in him.

He was beautiful like that, riding me with his long, strong legs spread wide over my hips and his lean muscles flexing with his motions. It was so much better than even the best daydream because he was right here, with me, arching into my touches and moaning my name.

Then his smooth moves became more erratic and more urgent, and I could tell he was close. I wasn't going to last much longer, either, and I doubled my efforts, and never mind the fact that my thighs started to burn and my lower back protested. But what's a little discomfort in comparison to the sight of Sherlock Holmes riding me? The sight of him cupping his own balls, squeezing and pulling? I'd gladly limp to work and with a smile, too.

He stiffened and with a desperate shout started shooting creamy jets that landed on my belly and chest. It was the hottest thing I had seen in a long time, and, as Sherlock's tight channel clenched and unclenched around me, I clamped my hands around his thighs, gathered my remaining strength and thrust into the tight heat until I felt my balls tighten and pull up. Sherlock fell forward to catch my broken sound with a kiss, and I clutched his shoulders and clung to him, and he kissed me with the exact same intensity as the orgasm that shot through me. Hot and hard and mind-blowing.

I'd never been kissed through an orgasm before, and it was the strangest and most intimate thing that had ever been done to me. Now, I'm not all that spiritual, but it felt like Sherlock was taking my soul from me and returning it the next instant, enriched with some of his own, and with what little part of my thinking brain was still working, I noticed we had entwined our hands as tightly as we had our bodies. And still we kissed, and still I twitched until all strength was gone, and I grew limp, just as if someone had pulled the plug on me.

Sherlock sat back on his heels but did not let go of my hands.

'You came,' he stated the obvious, and I managed a weak huff.

'I certainly did. As did you.'

'Mhm.'

He stayed where he was for a few more heartbeats as if he was contemplating something, and when he had reached his decision, he climbed off me and out of bed.

'Goodnight, John. I hope you'll sleep well tonight.'

And he was gone.

I propped myself up on an elbow and stared at the closed door. What the fuck? Then I flopped back and started laughing.

Goodnight, John indeed.

I removed the condom with shaking hands and dropped it to the floor. My hand brushed the sticky mess on my stomach, and I laughed some more. Trust Sherlock to rev me up, make a mess and leave it to me to clean up behind him.

'You're a little shit, Holmes,' I said into the darkness and fished for my boxers to wipe Sherlock's come off me. 'But a sexy little shit.'

When most of the goo was gone, I flung the boxers aside, turned around on my preferred side – left – and was fast asleep within seconds.

No bad dreams came to me that night.

CHAPTER NINETEEN

IT WAS POURING THE NEXT MORNING WHEN I CHECKED THE WEATHER FROM the bathroom window, but I didn't care. My thighs were a little sore, but I was fine with that. Guess it was safe to say I was feeling rather chipper that morning, and when I noticed a pale red spot on the curve of my neck I grinned at my reflection in the mirror. So he had left a mark after all! It wasn't a deep red bite mark that stood out like a beacon, but it was unmistakable nevertheless. No worries, though. I would simply button my polo shirt at work to avoid comments. I didn't generally mind but I wasn't quite ready to share this. Not yet.

I reached for my electric razor, changed my mind, and took out the straight razor, my badger brush, and the ridiculously expensive shaving cream I'd treated myself to a while ago. Getting laid by Sherlock called for a little indulging. Still grinning, I whipped the cream up in a small bowl until it had the desired frothy consistency and started lathering up.

A good, close shave later I left the bathroom, humming to myself, and dressed for work. When I went into the kitchen I found the breakfast table set and the coffee machine running, but my flatmate was nowhere near.

Shame. I'd like to have seen him before I left, if only to find out what he'd be like on the morning after. Would he be willing to talk about what had happened last night? Would he enlighten me about what on earth he had been thinking, coming to me the way he had?

Flattering – and embarrassing – as it was that the sound of me tossing off in the shower had turned him on, was it really the only reason?

I fed the boys and sat down with a buttered slice of toast and a cup of coffee and reached for my mobile. A message from Karim, letting me know he'd arrived in Dubai. Another one from Robbie, reminding me to use the new alarm codes, now that our new alarm system finally was in place.

Chewing on my toast, I typed a quick message to Karim.

Guess what. I got laid last night.

A reply came within seconds.

Don't do that, man. I'm about to see the senior sheikh.

Then...

Was it any good?

Mind-blowing. Brilliant. He's beautiful. Best sex I've had in ages. I came so hard I almost cried. I think I died a little. I think he might be the one.

The moment I hit 'send' I wished I hadn't. Wouldn't this–

THE FUCK???

–come across a bit too strong? I typed a quick PS.

Sorry about that. Post-coital high.

What did I tell you? He got under your skin.

Hope I didn't kill your vibe. Happy negotiating.

Fuck off.

I laughed and clicked on my favourite news app to flip through the headlines but found I wasn't able to concentrate. Much as I hated to admit it, Karim was right. In less than four months Sherlock had got under my skin and I couldn't imagine coming home to an empty flat any longer. Nor could I imagine coming home to anyone else.

Where was this headed?

'Mind if I join you for a cuppa?'

I turned around, coffee pot in hand. 'Good morning, Sherlock. Thanks for making breakfast.'

'You're welcome. Sorry I'm late, but I needed to look at something Mycroft sent me last night.'

He came over to stand next to me, and I briefly toyed with the idea of kissing him good morning. I poured him a cup instead. He thanked me with a nod and a smile and sat down at the table. Sat down a little carefully, I noticed out of the corner of my eye, and I couldn't quite suppress a self-satisfied smirk. Guess I wasn't the only one who'd been left with a souvenir.

'Want some toast?' I asked over my shoulder, trying to wipe the grin off my face.

'Just some flakes, please.'

'Regular or chocolate?'

'Regular.'

I poured a healthy portion into a bowl, added some milk and sat it down before him.

'Thanks,' he said and when he saw me put my plate into the dishwasher, added, 'Do you have to leave already?'

'In a few minutes, yes. My first patient's scheduled for 8.30, and I need to prepare the operating room.'

'Oh. Something bad?'

'No, only a few moles to remove.'

'I see.'

He fell silent and busied himself with his flakes. I turned to pour a second cup of coffee for myself when he cleared his throat.

'That was a good fuck last night. I needed that. Thank you.'

I turned around and stared at him. 'My pleasure,' I said. What else was there to say?

His cheeks turned pink, and he stirred his flakes with remarkable concentration.

I couldn't resist. 'I take it you weren't entirely displeased with my performance?'

'Not at all.' He raised his head and looked at me. 'I enjoyed it immensely. In fact, I was thinking–' He paused.

'Yes?' I encouraged.

'Would you, ah,' he cleared his throat, unexpectedly shy for someone who'd been so outspoken last night. 'What I mean is, would you mind terribly if we did that again?'

Would I – how about right now? Screw the moles. Robbie could take care of that just as well.

'Would you like that?' I asked instead.

'I would indeed,' he said.

I leaned against the sink, swirling my coffee. 'That could certainly be arranged.'

'Good.' He put a spoonful of flakes into his mouth and chewed. Then, 'I liked having your cock in me. It's good to be with a man who knows how to use the tools he's been given.'

I inhaled my coffee and started wheezing.

Sherlock frowned. 'What is it? Did I say something wrong?'

He sounded genuinely puzzled, and I wheezed some more. This post-sex talk was quickly turning from awkward to bizarre, and here I had thought I'd grown used to Sherlock's ways.

'You did not,' I finally managed, set my mug down and wiped my eyes. 'I just, uh, didn't expect that exact phrasing.'

'It was meant as a compliment.'

He sounded so earnest that I found it hard to keep a straight face. 'I hope you did. I rather enjoyed having my cock in you,' I replied. 'But why didn't you stay?'

'I wasn't sure that's what you wanted,' he said, chewing around a mouthful. 'I practically ambushed you and didn't want to impose on you anymore.'

'I liked being ambushed like that, and I would have liked you to stay.' I ventured for another sip of coffee. 'If you plan to do it again, please don't leave me when we're done. I quite enjoyed waking up with you in my bed that other morning.'

'I will keep that in mind. So, how was the meeting with Karim?'

'What? How did you know about that?'

He shot me a sideways glance. 'You smelled of ale.'

'I've been to the pub after work before. How does me smelling of ale tell you I was out with Karim and not with the practice team?'

'You took two steps at a time when you came home, which is something you very rarely do, unless you're feeling especially lighthearted.' He grinned. 'Also, you told me last night when you got home.'

'Oh, good. For a moment I thought you're a mindreader after all.'

'Don't be absurd.'

I shrugged a shoulder and finished my coffee. 'It was good. He told me they had to move the *Star Wars* watch-a-thon back by two weeks. You're invited, too.'

'Good heavens. All the movies?'

'The trilogies plus *Rogue One*. But maybe they'll have mercy, and it'll only be the original trilogy after all.'

'Is Djamal going to be there?'

'Yes. And a couple of other friends of theirs.'

'Good. That's very good.'

'Why is that good?' I looked at him. He averted his eyes. 'Are you jealous?' I asked, incredulous.

'I am not,' he said, a little too quickly.

I grinned. 'You are.'

'Mhm.'

'Don't be. Karim and I go back a long while. We went to uni together. He was reading economics and finance, I think, and I was a first-year medical student. We met on the rugby team and later shared a small flat for two semesters but that's it.'

'Did you, ah…'

'No, we did not. He's not my type and he likes his men beautiful.'

Sherlock scoffed at that and looked me over from head to toe. 'I don't understand what he thinks is missing.'

'Thank you,' I said. 'Other than that, we've been mates ever since.' I checked the clock above the kitchen door. 'Well, I better go.'

I put my mug into the dishwasher and went into the hallway to grab my messenger bag and put my shoes on. With my jacket in my hand, I paused at the door and strained my ears to check whether he'd get up from the breakfast table to say good-bye. All I heard was the sound of his spoon against the bowl and the rustle of the newspaper.

'Bye, Sherlock,' I called, still hoping for him to come and see me off. What I got was an absent-sounding 'bye,' and so I got my keys and went downstairs, disappointed.

Was this how it was going to be from now on? Thanks for the fuck and bye, John? True, I hadn't known what to expect when I got up this morning, and, true, he had left after sex, but he'd offered an acceptable explanation for that. I guess some part of my brain had hoped for a slight shift towards a more romantic, well, togetherness of sorts. Maybe I was still high on endorphins.

I got my bike out of its corner and rolled my trouser leg up, but when I unlocked the front door, I heard rapid steps galloping down the stairs.

'John, wait!'

I turned around. Sherlock came running towards me.

'Yes?'

He cupped my face and kissed me on the mouth, hard. When he let go, he smiled. 'See you tonight, John.'

My heart did a little flip. 'See you tonight, Sherlock.'

He nodded and ran back upstairs but paused on the last step, turned, and gave me a little wave.

I made the five-point-something miles to the practice in under 25 minutes that day.

Chapter Twenty

My workday flew by, and even Jen let herself be infected – to some degree – by my cheerful mood. She brought a coffee refill into my consulting room and set it down with one of her rare smiles.

'Here you go, John,' she said. 'Whatever you did, you should do it more often.'

She cast a meaningful glance to where Sherlock's mark sat, and my hand flew up. I'd completely forgotten to button my polo shirt and I hastily did. Jen's smile widened into a grin, and that was something *she* should do more often.

I grinned back. 'I intend to, Jen,' I stage-whispered. 'But don't tell anyone. It's too soon to make an announcement.'

'Understood,' she stage-whispered back and gave me a wink. 'If anyone asks, I'll say it's a mild rash. New washing powder.'

'Thank you. You're a darling.'

'Only when I choose to be.'

I barely made it through the team meeting, was out the door and on my bike in the blink of an eye, wove my way through the daily traffic jam with an ignorance hovering dangerously near reckless, and arrived home around 6.30.

Mrs Hudson was stepping out of the front door just as I got to a halt before 221B.

'Good evening, Mrs Hudson,' I greeted her and swung off the bike.

'Good evening, Dr Watson. How are you?'

'Very well, thank you.'

'Mr Holmes tells me you are happy with the flat.'

'We are indeed. What brings you here?' I ran a quick mental check for anything that might require a visit from our landlady.

'I sought Mr Holmes out on a matter of–' she hesitated. 'A personal matter.'

Sought out? As in, hired him? It seemed unlikely, given how he'd got her bristles up when we'd looked at the flat, but then again, that had been a while ago, we were paying our rent on time, and Sherlock could be a charmer when he chose to be.

'Ah,' I said. 'I hope he was able to help you.'

She gave a non-committal shrug. 'We've only just spoken. He promised to look into the matter.'

'I see.'

She walked down the short flight of stairs, and I shouldered my bike.

'Have a pleasant evening, Mrs Hudson.'

'Thank you.'

THE DOOR TO THE flat was yanked open just as I reached the last step, and Sherlock all but hauled me inside.

'I thought she'd never leave,' he said, kicked the door shut, and pushed me against the wall. 'Hello, John. How was your day?'

'Fine–' I began but Sherlock pressed his mouth on mine. I let my messenger bag slide to the floor, pulled him closer, and forced his lips open with my tongue. He made a sound deep in his throat, pushed my jacket off my shoulders, grabbed my shirt and my undershirt with both hands, and pulled them over my head, breaking the kiss only for the short time it took to divest me of my clothes, then glued himself to my mouth again.

I laughed softly against his lips, delighted and aroused by his impatience. So what if I didn't understand his motivation for seeking me out the way he did and maybe – probably – I'd go back to wondering about what it was exactly he wanted from me, but right now I had no objection to being used to satisfy his physical needs. Lord knows I had needs, too, and now that I'd finally had a taste of Sherlock I couldn't get enough.

And so I unbuttoned and unzipped his trousers, slid my hands into his waistband and around his hips, reached for his taut buttocks, and pulled him against me, letting him feel how much I wanted him, too.

'You're so fucking hot.' I licked across his throat and lightly bit his Adam's apple, then licked and bit his stubborn chin, which made him laugh. It was a deep, throaty laugh, much like his brother's, but Sherlock's laugh was a lot sexier, and it shot right to my cock. I grabbed him tighter, pulled his buttocks apart, and tapped against his hole with my middle finger. His laughter turned into a moan and he rubbed himself against me.

'I want your cock in me, John. I could think about little else all day.' His eyes were very dark, his irises but a narrow blue-and-grey ring around his huge pupils. 'I've not been able to get much work done.'

'My apologies.'

'It was bloody distracting. I kept seeing you and how you looked when I rode you.' He opened the fly of my jeans, button by button, and his hand found my cock, rubbing me through my boxer briefs.

'So beautiful,' he whispered. 'So hard.' He reached inside my briefs, pumped me, once, twice, and I let my head fall back against the wall. 'Fuck me again, John.'

Oh, he was gorgeous when he talked dirty.

'Bedroom?' I asked tentatively and was rewarded with a grin so wide it could have lit the entire street. Sherlock pulled me across the hall and into my bedroom where I quickly switched on the reading lamp. We stripped quickly and unceremoniously, shedding denim and cotton with a few swift moves, unwilling to wait another second and not interested in the fine art of seduction.

I pulled him into my arms and let myself fall backwards onto my bed, taking him with me. With a quick move, I rolled us around so that he came to lie on his back, underneath me.

'And this,' I said and kissed the corners of his mouth, 'is what I've been thinking about all day. You, in my bed.'

'Naked and about to bottom out for you?'

He made it sound slightly reproachful, but the laughter in his eyes gave him away, and I gently bit his lower lip.

'Smart deduction, that.'

'Bossy, huh.'

'Years of being in command will do that to you.'

'What rank?'

'Captain.'

'Captain Watson.' There was a note of satisfaction in his voice, and I propped myself up on my elbows.

'You don't have a military kink, do you?'

'What would you do if I said yes?'

He gasped when I bit down on his shoulder. 'You're a horrible tease, you know that, yeah?'

I slid down, leaving a trail of kisses and bites, licked and nibbled my way across his ribcage, blew gently across his navel, which made him laugh and try to squirm away, but I held him ruthlessly in place.

Sherlock's breath became more laboured the farther I went down, and a whimpering sound escaped his lips when I licked along his shaft in one swift stroke, lapping at the moist tip, and he covered his mouth in embarrassed mortification.

I looked up and lightly slapped his wrists.

'Why so shy all of a sudden? Let me hear you, Sherlock. Let me know I'm doing it right.'

He nodded silently, and I closed my lips around the tip of his cock and sucked it into my mouth an inch at a time.

He was gorgeous like that, with his head flung back into my pillow, his hands clawing at the sheets and his long legs spread wide, giving himself over to pleasure. He smelled great, too, a mixture of lust and body wash and Sherlock, and it drove all else from my mind.

'Oh God yes, yes John,' he panted. 'Please. John. Dear God. I'm close. Please.'

I placed both hands on his hips and sucked his cock deep into my mouth, letting him feel my throat work around him. It had been a while since I'd last deep-throated anyone, and I worried about retching when I first swallowed him whole but much to my delight – and to his – I could still do it. I guess it's a little like riding a bike.

Sherlock fisted the bedsheets, and I looked up into his face. Our eyes met and locked, and then his hips jerked up convulsively, and he came in hot spurts. I sucked in time to every pulse, swallowing it all and prolonging the sensation until Sherlock pulled away.

'Stop, for heaven's sake, John, please stop,' he half laughed, half begged. I licked my lips and slowly slid up his body until we were at eye level again.

'Pleased?'

'Mhm.' Sherlock stretched languorously. 'And now please fuck me.'

'You sure? Don't you need a minute to, uhm, recover?'

'Yes. But I want you more. So hurry before I change my mind.'

And so I hurried to reach across him and opened the drawer of my bedside table to pull out lube and condoms.

'Ready when you are.'

Sherlock took the lube bottle out of my hands and snapped the lid open. 'What's taking so long?'

Never before had I slipped a condom on quite so quickly, and Sherlock grinned when I held out my right hand. He tilted the bottle to squirt a generous amount of lube into my palm, then watched me slick my cock. Despite its current spent state Sherlock's prick responded with an interested twitch.

'Patience,' I said with a calm that was entirely dishonest. 'Let me make this right for you.'

'You are making this right.' He took the lube bottle away from me. 'Please, John. Now.'

I looked down into his face and without another word aligned my cock and started pushing inside, slowly and carefully.

'I don't think I'll last,' I whispered. 'You're perfect, so fucking perfect and tight and beautiful, and I want you so, so much.'

I buried my face in the curve of his neck and tried to get myself back under control, then pulled out until only the tip of my cock was buried inside the tight opening and pushed back in, slowly, drawing it out for as long as possible. I slid my hand along Sherlock's thigh until I reached the hollow of his knee and drew his leg up a little. Sherlock shifted and wrapped his leg around my hips, pulling me closer, inviting me to go deeper. After a few more slow strokes I lost myself in his heat and set a pace that had him cry out and arch his back.

Then it all became a white-hot mess inside my head, hell, my whole system became one white-hot mess, I lost my rhythm, and with a last, desperate thrust I shouted my release.

When I was spent, I dropped on top of Sherlock who caught my dead weight in a sure embrace.

'Come here, you,' he said and kissed the tip of my nose. 'That was amazing.'

'I aim to please,' I murmured and rolled off him to lie on my side and removed the condom, feeling the familiar post-coital sleepiness spreading throughout my body. 'Will you stay with me tonight, Sherlock?'

He made a non-committal sound.

'Please?'

The look in his eyes was impossible to read, especially in my dazed state of mind, but then he shrugged, fumbled for the blanket and pulled it up and over both of us.

'If that's what you want.'

'It is,' I said sleepily and yawned. 'It is.'

I woke up in the middle of the night, needing to piss. One of Sherlock's arms was flung across my chest, and I carefully wriggled out from underneath it, not wanting to wake him.

After doing what needed to be done I looked at myself in the mirror and grinned. My muscles hurt in the most pleasant way, and there was a bright red mark on my shoulder. I touched it, and my grin spread wider as I remembered the feeling of Sherlock's lips and teeth on my skin as he had bitten and sucked it into existence.

I switched off the light and hurried back into the bedroom to slip back into bed.

Sherlock had turned to lie on his stomach but immediately turned towards me, mumbled something unintelligible and again flung his arm across my chest. I shifted a little and tentatively put my arm up and around him. He shuffled closer, put his head on my shoulder and heaved a deep sigh, threw a leg over mine, and there I was, half covered by a sleeping police consultant. I smiled and with my free hand pulled the blanket up again.

When I woke up to the sound of my alarm clock, Sherlock was gone.

Chapter Twenty-One

The phone call came on Monday.

I was going through my afternoon schedule after a quick lunch. It was mainly routine stuff I was to look at, two surgery aftercare cases, a check-up on a patient with a knee replacement that had been giving him problems, and two hours for walk-in cases.

My mobile rang just before my second patient was admitted inside. It was an unknown number, and although I made a point of not answering unknown callers on my private phone while I was at work, I answered that one.

Looking back, I think it was a classic case of gut instinct, a vague premonition of something not being right.

'John Watson,' I said.

There was a short pause at the other end.

'Who is this?'

'This is Djamal.'

'Oh, hello Djamal,' I checked my watch and leaned back in my chair. 'I'm at the practice, and the next patient is due any minute so I can't speak for more than a few moments. What can I do for you?'

'I see. I'm sorry to disturb you but–' there was an audible swallow and a sound I couldn't place, then Djamal cleared his throat. 'I have very bad news.'

'What is it?' I sat up straight.

'Karim...Karim's dead, John.'

'What?'

There was that sound again, and now I recognised it. It was a suppressed sob.

'Karim's dead,' Djamal repeated, his voice breaking on the word 'dead'.

'But...how? When? He texted me–'

I looked at my phone and called up Karim's last message, '–he texted on Friday, saying he scored in Dubai and was not looking forward to the team thing.'

'He was shot during laser tag.'

'What?' I noticed I was shouting and lowered my voice.

'How can you get shot during laser tag? Isn't that like paintball with fancy lights?'

'The police are looking into that,' Djamal said. 'John, can I come and see you? I must talk about this with someone or I'll go mad.'

'Of course. I get off work at – no, fuck that. Just swing by. Come by right now if you want. I'll shift my appointments around. You have the address?'

'No. I found your number on Karim's list but he didn't write down an address.'

'What list?'

'His emergency list.' Djamal cleared his throat again. 'You know, whom to call if anything happened. Your name is second, after his sister's.'

'I – uh,' now it was my voice that threatened to break, and I did some throat-clearing myself. 'Of course.' I gave him the address. 'It's near London Bridge station.'

'I'm on my way. Thank you, John.'

'Don't mention it,' I said mechanically. 'See you in a bit.'

We rang off and I stared at the cheerful photo at the opposite wall, head swimming and thoughts frozen.

Karim was dead? Karim who'd tell me to fuck off and wish for Allah's blessing upon my soul in one breath? How was that even possible?

The door opened and Jen swanned inside with the file of my next patient.

'Here you go, John,' she said. 'Mr Bellings has just arrived with his latest blood results.' She narrowed her eyes and gave me a sharp look. 'Anything the matter?'

I blinked up at her. 'May I have a few minutes, please? I just had some very bad news.'

'Oh.' She frowned. 'Anything concerning your–' she made a vague gesture, 'your friend?'

'What?' I asked, not understanding. 'Oh. No. Not him. But somebody very close to me.'

'Of course. I'll tell Mr Bellings you have to make a phone call.'

'Thank you, Jen. I appreciate that.'

And I did. Ever since she'd spotted Sherlock's bite mark, our Jen had gone a little softer on me. Not that she'd favoured me or overlooked my administrative failings, of which there were many, as she repeatedly told me, but she'd lost most of her waspishness and smiled a little more often. She gave me an understanding smile now and left my room.

I got up from my chair and walked over to the wall where my certificates were lined up to stare at the one from university. Images and memories of Karim teasing me for being such a slow runner tumbled through my head, of his easy smile and foul mouth, of how he had picked me up on my release from the military hospital...but most of all I remembered how he had held me after I had woken from nightmare after nightmare.

Pain surged through me, real, physical pain that constricted my throat and threatened to burst my chest and I bent forward, placed my hands on my knees and grit my teeth in an effort to hold back a sob. After a few moments of controlled breathing I straightened, squared my shoulders and opened the door.

'Mr Bellings,' I greeted my next patient. 'I'm sorry for keeping you waiting, but there was a phone call I had to make.' I gestured for him to get inside. 'Please, come. I understand you brought your latest lab results?'

'I did, yes.' Bellings handed me an envelope. 'The surgeon says it's all going as is to be expected, but I wanted to hear your opinion, Dr Watson.'

'Of course.' I closed the door. 'Please take a seat.'

DJAMAL SAT WAITING OUTSIDE my room when I returned from the operating room where I'd stitched together a small household accident. Thinking it best to keep the personal connection to ourselves for the moment, I held out my hand.

'Dr John Watson,' I said. 'We spoke on the phone earlier.'

He caught on and took my hand. 'Djamal Mokhtari. Thank you for seeing me at such short notice, Dr Watson.'

I opened the door to my room and gestured for him to step inside, then put up the 'Do not disturb' sign. The staff knew better than to interrupt without knocking, but I wanted to make absolutely sure.

Out of the corner of my eyes I saw Jen coming out of Sheila's office, and I gave her a nod. She understood at once and nodded back. With Jen guarding my door, our privacy was secured. Nobody but the Queen herself was going to be granted access, and I wasn't sure even Her Majesty would be allowed to touch the door-handle without Jen checking back with me first.

I closed the door.

'Djamal,' I said. 'What on earth happened?'

He swayed, and for a moment I was afraid his knees were going to give. I pulled up a chair, and he sat down heavily. I sat down opposite him, and we looked at each other. For a while, neither of us spoke a word.

'You really are handsome,' Djamal finally said and I blinked.

'What?'

'You're a very handsome man,' he repeated and gave a short laugh. It sounded more like a bark than a laugh. 'Karim talked a lot about you and showed me tons of photos of the two of you. You have no idea how jealous that made me. It got a bit better after I met you but still…'

'Why would you be jealous?'

'Because you know each other so well. Knew each other,' he corrected himself and just like that, the iron grip he must have had on himself crumpled before my eyes and he bent over, much like I had, hung his head between his knees and folded his hands over the back of his head, as if he was trying to protect himself from a blow.

I reached out and placed a hand on one of his knees.

'Djamal,' I gently said. 'Will you not tell me what happened?'

I heard him take a laboured breath, then he sat up and wiped his eyes.

'I can't tell you much more than what I said over the phone,' he said in a trembling voice. 'He went to that teambuilding thing they had scheduled. There was to be laser tag on Saturday and some group discussions with a management consultant on Sunday morning. They were all booked into a hotel, and he told me he wasn't going to be available because they had to hand in their phones during the active sessions to make it a real group experience.'

'What? Karim without his mobile?'

'I know,' Djamal said with a weak chuckle. 'Inconceivable, isn't it?'

'I always thought it would have to be surgically removed one day.'

'And was he angry about having to give it up. A violation of his bloody personality rights, he called it.'

I laughed despite all. 'Sounds just like him.'

'Anyway, I was at my brother's, celebrating the birth of his daughter. Finally, a girl after three boys. Tarek is so proud of his little princess, and the whole family was there, so I was too busy to be worried about not hearing from Karim.'

'So how did you find out?'

'Phoebe rang me. She's his work wife, the one who went to Dubai with him, and she's the only one in his company who knew about us.'

I nodded. I'd heard of Phoebe and knew how much Karim had respected and liked her.

'She said–' he swallowed and his eyes became suspiciously bright. He blinked rapidly, then continued, 'She said when their round ended, both teams met by the results board, but Karim was missing. They waited for a while, thinking he'd gone to the loo using one of the back exits but when he didn't show, they went in search of him. They found him... They found him lying behind one of the cardboard rocks. He was shot, John. Karim was shot.'

He started sobbing, and I felt my throat tighten up. I didn't know what to say or do. Really, what was there to say or do?

'Have you spoken to the police yet?' I finally asked.

'Not yet, but I'm sure they'll come to see me sooner or later. As soon as they go through his phone records.'

'In that case, they'll probably come to see me, too,' I said. 'We've talked and texted a lot these past weeks.'

'I know,' Djamal said, sniffing. I pushed a Kleenex box his way, and he took one, blew his nose and continued, 'He told me you and Sherlock were coming over for the *Star Wars* weekend.'

We looked at each other, the words *not going to happen now* hanging between us.

I honestly cannot remember what else we spoke about, but when Djamal left, I made him promise to call me anytime he needed to talk. I wasn't entirely certain he'd do it, but he nodded, gave me his number in return, and I saved it to my phone.

There would probably be a few phone calls and maybe one or two meetings, three at the most, during which we'd share memories, but then we'd each go our separate ways. Wasn't that always the case? You bond over the death of a loved one, but unless you've known each other before, it's a short-lived bond that's bound to vanish once the most painful stage of grieving is behind you.

Part of me hoped it was going to be different with Djamal. He was the man who had made Karim happy during the past couple of months, and I guess I thought if we kept in touch, Karim would stay with us.

Chapter Twenty-Two

When I got home, I found Sherlock perching on the back of his favourite armchair, engaged in a heated, if somewhat one-sided, discussion with a middle-aged man in a greyish suit.

'Really, Gregson,' Sherlock was saying in a voice usually heard around very stubborn children, 'you must learn to observe more closely. It's obvious from the amount of attention she's paying to signs and portents she's a superstitious woman, and I therefore consider it highly unlikely she would walk under a ladder. Therefore, she cannot have "scurried by unnoticed", as you put it, because she would have walked in bright sunlight and not been sheltered by the shade of the wall.

'Which is a far-fetched theory in itself because the shade provided at that time of day is neither wide nor dark enough to conceal a grown woman, petite or no. Good evening, John,' he said, making the greeting sound as if it was part of the deduction he'd just been walking the other man through.

'Gregson needs to talk to you about something and wanted to meet you at the surgery, but I told him you usually come home between six and seven, and we had something to discuss anyway.'

'You mean you had something to tell me,' Gregson said and got up. 'I can't remember discussing anything for the last 10 minutes. Good evening, Dr Watson. I believe we haven't met yet. I'm Detective Inspector Gregson.'

'He works with Lestrade,' Sherlock supplied.

'Good evening, Inspector.' I eyed his suit and tie and how he had shifted from slightly annoyed but politely listening to brisk and official and knew what he wanted to talk about. 'I take it this is not a social call?'

'Indeed it is not,' he confirmed and cast a sideways look at Sherlock who had slid down from the back of his armchair and was now sitting cross-legged.

'He may stay,' I answered the unspoken question. 'He'll find out soon enough.'

'Very well.' Gregson sat back down and took out his notepad. 'How well are you acquainted with a certain Karim Halabi, Dr Watson?'

'We met during our university years. He was a good friend.'

Sherlock's eyes widened by a mere fraction.

'*Was* a good friend, Dr Watson?' Gregson gave me a sharp look.

'I learnt about his death earlier this afternoon so yes, *was* a good friend.'

'May I ask how you came into possession of this knowledge?'

'I received a phone call from Mr Djamal Mokhtari, a close friend of Karim. After we spoke on the phone he dropped by the surgery to speak with me in person.'

'And how well do you know Mr Mokhtari?'

'We met for dinner once. With Karim and Sherlock.'

'I see.' Gregson scribbled something down. 'And how would you describe your relationship with the deceased?'

'Like I said, we met during university. We played rugby on the same team, shared an apartment for a while, and have been friends ever since.'

'That's all?'

'I don't understand, Inspector.'

I understood very well, but I wanted him to spell it out for me.

'Has your friendship ever exceeded the boundaries of mere friendship?'

'Have we ever been in a relationship, you mean? No.'

'So you never–'

'No.' I met Gregson's dubious gaze with a raised eyebrow. 'There's friendship amongst gay men, too, Inspector. Contrary to what the public is being fed about our "alternative lifestyle", I made sure the quotation marks were audible, 'we don't all hump each other.'

'I didn't mean to offend,' Gregson hastened to assure me.

'I'm sure you didn't. It needed to be said nevertheless.'

'Very well. So, when did you last see Mr Halabi?'

'Last Wednesday. We met for a pint at the *Broken Drum*.'

'What did you talk about?'

'He reminded me of the movie weekend he had invited me to, that he had just successfully closed a business deal, or was about to, and that he wasn't looking forward to the upcoming team event.'

Gregson flipped through his notes. 'The laser tag?'

'That is correct.'

He asked me a couple more questions – what mood had Karim been in, what kind of impression had he given, had he sounded worried about anything, was I aware of enemies he might have had.

I answered to my best of abilities. He had been exhausted from work but overall cheerful. He'd been pleased about the outcome of his latest deal but irked at something he'd found in some calculation. No enemies that I was aware of.

And then, the inevitable question.

'Where were you between 2 and 5pm last Saturday, Dr Watson?'

'At home, with Sherlock.'

'Doing what?'

Fucking him into the mattress.

'Domestic chores,' I said without flinching. 'You know, laundry, cleaning, and the like.'

'I see.' He looked over at Sherlock. 'Can you confirm that, Mr Holmes?'

'Yes,' Sherlock said. 'He was with me all afternoon. The rest of the day, too.'

'I went to the gym around eleven,' I added. 'I'll give you the address and my membership number, so you can have my login and logout times checked. After that, I went to pick up some groceries and came straight home. I think I still have the receipt from the shop, if you want it.'

'That would be helpful.'

I went to fetch my wallet, and, yes, the receipt was still there. I handed it to Gregson who looked at it and scribbled something down. He wrote down the gym details, too, and finally rose to leave.

'Thank you for your time, Dr Watson. We will need your official statement at New Scotland Yard at your earliest convenience.'

'Certainly. Will tomorrow afternoon be early enough? I have two surgeries scheduled for tomorrow morning.'

'Of course.' He handed me his card. 'If anything else comes to mind, please ring me up.'

'Will do.'

'Ladder,' Sherlock shouted after us as I escorted him to the door. 'Have the entry wound checked and the angle re-examined.'

'Yes, yes,' muttered Gregson and shouted back, 'Thanks for your input, Holmes. I'll set the team to it.' He turned to me. 'I'm sorry for the loss of your friend, Dr Watson, and please understand I had to ask those questions.'

'That's all right. It takes more than that to offend me.'

'Glad to hear it.' He held out his hand. 'Have a nice evening.'

We shook hands and he left. I watched him walk down the flight of stairs, and, when he pulled the front door closed behind him, I went back into the living room where Sherlock still sat cross-legged in his armchair. He looked up from his mobile.

'Everything all right, John?'

I shook my head. 'Nothing's all right.'

He motioned as if to say something, but I held up my hand.

'Not now, Sherlock. Please.'

He nodded and went back to typing away on his phone.

I went into my room, kicked off my shoes and lay down on my bed to stare at the ceiling, waiting for sleep, or tears, or anger. Anything, really, anything to make the truth sink in or better yet: convince me this was another of my really bad dreams.

Karim dead? Not possible. We hadn't got to see each other as much as we used to, his working hours being as crazy as they were and me doing more volunteer work than I had originally planned for, but we'd never really fallen out of touch, nor did I think we ever would. Would have. Would have had. Whatever.

How could he be dead? How did anyone get shot during laser tag? Who would do such a thing? Why did people shoot other people? Lord knows I had shot and killed, but that had been during war, in a combat situation. Not that those lives had meant any less, but...

This wasn't going anywhere helpful.

I got up and changed into my running gear because whenever I needed to get something out of my system or when I was chewing on a problem that wouldn't solve itself, I went for a run, a habit I'd picked up when I was a teenager.

Karim's death didn't really fall into either category, but I hoped running would take some of the pain away. Or yank me out of the pointless thought spiralling I was about to fall into. Just leave it all behind for a couple of miles.

And so I ran along Baker Street and over to Regent's Park.

I WAS DRENCHED IN sweat when I got back, and my leg sent clear messages to my brain that it had been a shit idea to run at this pace and for this long, too. Sherlock was nowhere in sight, but I heard his voice from upstairs. He sounded all off, and I stopped to listen. It took me a moment but then I figured out he sounded different because he wasn't speaking English. Was that Chinese? Could be, with all of the hissing and 'shurrrr' sounds. I'd have to ask him about that, but not now. I was not in the mood to ask anything.

I crawled into bed after a quick shower, and, when sleep finally came, it was anything but a peaceful slumber. I heard gunshots and explosions. I heard my mates crying for help. I ran and ran but I was too far away and I would never reach them in time. But then there was Karim, holding out his hand for me to hang on to.

But – what was he doing here? Karim had no reason to be here. He'd never served in the military and, as far as I knew, he'd never set foot into Afghanistan.

'Take my hand, John,' he called out to me and I reached for him, closing my hand around his wrist. He pulled me against his chest and I clung to him and it was all good. It was all good.

'You're here,' I said, nearly sobbing with relief. 'You're here.'

'Of course I'm here, John. Where else would I be?'

'I thought you're dead. Djamal told me you were shot.'

'I'm not dead yet,' said a voice that sounded like Karim and not like him at all. 'I will die eventually but so far I'm still here.'

My eyelids seemed to weigh a ton each, and I struggled to open my eyes, caught in that horrible vacuum where you feel trapped within your own body, where your consciousness is stirring back to life but your body is still asleep. I heard panicked sounds coming from somewhere. They were coming from my throat, I was the one making those noises because I was trapped and would soon be dead, too, dead just like Karim was dead–

'Shhh, John, it's all good,' said the Karim-not-Karim voice. 'I'm here. Wake up, John, it's all good.'

I woke with a start, heart pounding in my ears, feeling disoriented and dazed, but then my brain signalled I was safe, I wasn't trapped at all. It was Sherlock's arms wrapped around me, not some unknown foe's trying to suffocate me.

'You were dreaming, John. I heard you call out, and I came.' He loosened his embrace; moved as if to pull back but I reached for him.

'Please don't go. I don't–' I swallowed. *Say it.* 'I don't want to be alone now.' I buried my face in the curve of his neck. 'Please, Sherlock. Please.'

'All right.'

He pulled me back into his arms, and I let myself be held and inhaled the unique scent of him, that mixture of the body wash he liked, a hint of coffee, spearmint, and a faint whiff of cigarette smoke, which usually was a sure turn-off for me, but, with Sherlock, I didn't mind. He didn't smoke a lot and never in the flat, and he didn't exactly reek of tobacco, either. It was more of a faint echo, the grain of salt to remind you nothing is ever perfect, and so I inhaled deeply and listened to the soothing and incoherent nothings he mumbled into my hair and relaxed into his comforting warmth.

More often than I cared to remember I had woken from a nightmare like this and found myself all alone. Adam, my ex, had freaked out each time and bolted from the bedroom as if he'd woken up next to a monster. He wasn't an uncaring person, far from it, but he couldn't handle anything unpleasant near his personal space, and, looking back, I think it was the nightmares that eventually drove us apart, not my missing fashion sense or my ignorance where *Britain's Got Talent* was concerned.

But Sherlock was here. He'd come when he'd heard me, had not turned away, leaving me alone.

I nuzzled the side of his neck, and he tilted his head to the side, a wordless invitation, and I accepted without hesitation. It's an old cliché, isn't it, the need to fuck after being subjected to massive stress and tension, but as with all clichés, there's truth in this one, too.

I ground against him and found him hard.

'Yes,' he whispered, and 'Yes,' I whispered back.

That night, fucking felt like making love. It was slow and unhurried, with kisses and more nuzzling, with whispering and sighs, soft stroking, and soft moans, nose rubbing against nose and kisses and more kisses. Feathery-light, deep and hot, nibbling and playing. It was as if we had to make up for years of missed kissing. I felt his moan vibrate against my lips when I kissed the pulsing hollow at the base of this throat, just where he liked it, and he tugged at my hair, beckoning for me to slide up, his lips finding mine once more, firm and sweet, and he kissed me again, and we savoured every moment.

When I was finally seated deep inside him, I was shuddering with lust and longing. The heat of his body coursed down the entire length of mine, and I began to move, and he moved with me, and we soon found a tempo that matched our desire. It was slow and steady at first, picking up speed along the way, but it was nowhere near as hard and rough as our previous fucks had been. It was, well, yes – it was love-making.

When I came, I could not have said where my body ended and his began. I spilled into him, and it felt as if I was spilling parts of myself along with my come, and out of a still functioning corner of my mind I felt him twitch and jerk against my stomach, his long legs wrapped around my hips, his hands buried in my hair.

And finally, my tears came. I tried to turn away in a weak attempt to hide, but Sherlock pulled me back into his arms and held me through my tears just as he had held me through my orgasm, and I found I was not ashamed to show my pain and grief because this was Sherlock, and with him there was no need to ever be ashamed.

He left me only to fetch a damp flannel, and it was then that I realised I had forgotten to use a condom.

'Sherlock, we didn't–' I began, but he put a finger across my lips.

'I know we didn't, John,' he said and handed me the flannel. 'We'll talk about this tomorrow, yes?' He waited for me to finish, cleaned himself, and flung the flannel aside, then climbed back into bed.

'Tell me about Karim. I'm really sorry that I didn't get to know him better. What was he like?'

And so I talked about Karim and how we had met, quoted some of his favourite swearword combinations, cried some more, and eventually fell asleep with Sherlock's tall frame wrapped around me protectively, something I might have laughed about at any other time because I usually didn't feel like I needed protecting, but it felt comfortable, being the small spoon for a change.

That night, Sherlock stayed.

Chapter Twenty-Three

I WENT TO THE POLICE STATION THE NEXT AFTERNOON TO DELIVER MY statement, just as I had promised. Gregson had me sign the paperwork, added the usual phrases about how I should get in touch if I could think of anything else, and I was dismissed.

On the way out I ran into Lestrade, who balanced two large binders and a coffee mug, a deep crease between her brows.

'Good afternoon, Dr Watson,' she said. 'What brings you here?'

'A friend of mine was shot,' I said. 'Gregson needed my statement.'

'The Halabi case?' Her frown deepened. 'He was your friend?'

When I nodded, the crease disappeared some and she gave me a sympathetic look. 'I'm sorry for your loss.'

'Thank you. But I don't want to keep you, Inspector. You look busy.'

She made a face. 'I am. Team meeting in five. Sorry about that.'

'No need to apologise. It's not your job to keep people entertained.'

'Wish you'd tell that to the boss,' she muttered, raised her cup in greeting and turned to go. 'Oh, one more thing.'

I stopped and looked back.

'Tell your flatmate if he pulls one more stunt like he did this morning, I will break both his thumbs.'

That made me laugh despite all. 'Why, what has he done now?'

'I'm not at liberty to share, ongoing investigation, et cetera, but suffice to say it included a couple of smart text messages. I don't appreciate my team being ridiculed.'

'I see. I will tell him.'
'You do that.'

But there was something else I needed to talk about first, over dinner later, and it included a forgotten condom and safe sex practices.

'Oh, that,' Sherlock said when I approached the subject later that day over an assortment of takeaway Thai food. 'Don't worry too much about it, John.'

'I'm not particularly worried, Sherlock, but don't you think we should–'

'All done.'

He reached for his mobile, scrolled through his messages until he found what he was looking for, clicked something open, and handed me the phone.

'What's this?'

'Really, Dr Watson, as a physician you should recognise it for what it is.'

'I see what it is, but I don't understand.' The document stated somebody's blood test results. I scrolled up until I saw the patient's name. 'Oh. It's yours.'

'All good.'

'When did you get tested?'

'Two days ago.'

'How on earth did you get your results back so quickly?'

He raised his eyebrows. 'I know people who do stuff.'

'Uh-huh.' I returned the phone to him, and he pocketed it. 'But these are yours and mine are–'

'You had your routine check-up a month ago,' he said. 'A clean slate, pure as fallen snow.'

'How did you – did you hack my medical records?'

Why did I even bother asking? The answer was written all over his face.

'I know – well.' He had the grace to look remorseful. 'Maybe I shouldn't have done it, but I didn't want to wait for you to make up your mind when the time was right to go bareback. I guess an apology is in order, yes?'

I shrugged. I should be angry, furious even for having my privacy invaded like that and out of a whim, too, but I was tired and heartbroken, and when I looked at him and his half apologetic, half impish grin I found I didn't have any strength left to be angry. But it reminded me of something else.

'I ran into Lestrade when I was at the Met,' I said and helped myself to some more Moo Ping. 'She asked me to let you know she'd break your thumbs, both of them, if you ever repeat what you did this morning.'

'Dear me,' he said with mock alarm. 'Now I'm scared.'

'What did you do?' I asked between bites.

'I pointed a few things out to the investigating bunch. Really, it was nothing serious.'

'She mentioned something about your ridiculing her team.'

'Oh, that.' He snorted dismissively. 'No harm done. She's an even bigger mother hen than you are, John.'

'A mother hen who threatened to break your thumbs. Doesn't sound motherly to me.'

'You said you'd bust my kneecaps if I involved Bodie and Doyle in an experiment. Not very motherly either.'

'Yeah, whatever. Anyway,' I fished for a piece of Toong Tong but it fell off my chopsticks on the way from the box to my mouth. Sherlock sniggered. I glared at him, grabbed the elusive piece with my fingers and stuffed it into my mouth.

'Anyway,' I continued, chewing, 'I wish she was the officer in charge. I don't know what to make of Gregson. Not only did he ask me all kinds of stupid questions about the gay lifestyle, but he went all over the place trying to get me to admit that, yes, of course, Karim and I were fuck buddies after all, for that's what gays do, yeah? They fuck like rabbits. All the time.' I speared another Toong Tong.

Sherlock huffed. 'Don't get all worked up over Gregson, John,' he said. 'He's not worth it. He'll never rise above average, no matter how hard he tries to get into the DCI's good books. He just doesn't have it in him, and I sincerely hope the DCI is smart enough to see Lestrade is the better officer by far.'

'You like her, don't you?'

'I do, yes,' Sherlock admitted after some thoughtful chewing. 'She needs to work on her overall observational skills, as most people do, but she catches on quickly and isn't too stubborn to ask for help. She's a good team leader, as far as I can tell, and she's a fearsome kendoka.'

'She practises Kendo, too?'

'She received the sixth dan last year and earned the title of renshi in addition.'

'And that's good?'

'That's very good.'

'Do you hold a title?'

'No. But I'm training for the fourth dan.'

'What? Are you telling me she outranks you in the ring?'

He stuck his tongue out. 'She's older than I am, she's been practising since she was a teenager, and I don't think she's ever paused. With the exception of her pregnancies, that is.'

'And you have? Paused, I mean?'

'Well,' he said, a little evasively, 'let's just say there's been unstable times in my life.'

'Oh yeah? In what sense?'

'That's another story and shall be told another time. Anyway, third dan it is at the moment.'

I decided not to prod. I'd find out sooner or later. 'So, do you train with her?'

'Whenever I get the chance. Whenever I need to get my arse kicked,' he added with a grin.

Lestrade's kudos account went up a few more notches.

GREGSON'S, ON THE OTHER HAND, didn't. I rang him a few days later because there was indeed something I remembered.

'Karim said there was something fishy about one of the models he had prepared for an upcoming deal. No, not fishy. I think *odd* was the word he used,' I told Gregson over the phone.

'The models? What do models have to do with banking?'

'Not that kind of model. That's what they call their Excel sheets, you know, the fancy number crunching.'

'I see,' Gregson said, but it was obvious from his tone he really didn't. 'And what exactly was odd about the numbers?'

'I don't know. Karim never shared confidential company information with outsiders.'

'How would you know?'

'I would know because that's how he was, Inspector. Loyal and trustworthy. He would tell me if there was something gnawing at him, but if it was a business-related issue he wouldn't share the details. He thought there was something in one of his document folders that didn't belong, but that's all I know.'

'I see. I will have my team look into it.'

'Thank you,' I said politely and rang off. I drummed a nervous rap on my desk with my fingers, then scrolled for Djamal's number. He picked up on the second ring.

'Yes?'

'Djamal, hi, it's John.'

'Oh hello, John.' His voice sounded rough, and he cleared his throat. 'How are you?'

'All right, I guess. How are you?'

'Very well,' he said automatically, then gave a little, constricted laugh and said, 'No. I feel like shit. You caught me having a cry. A proper little girl, eh?'

'Bollocks,' I said bluntly. 'You've just lost someone very close to you, and there's no shame in crying.'

'Mhm.' He didn't sound convinced.

'Say, Djamal, have you spoken to the police again? Since giving your statement, I mean?'

'I have, yes. Why are you asking?'

'Because I just rang Gregson, and I had the impression he wasn't particularly interested. I mean, I don't expect the police to call in the cavalry just because some friend of the murder victim–'

Saying the words felt like cutting myself with a dull blade.

I took a breath. 'Because a friend calls with a boring little detail. But he sounded like: *uh-huh, next.* Know what I mean?'

'I know exactly what you mean,' Djamal said, and the anger in his voice made him sound more like himself again. 'I dropped by twice to add something to the statement I gave.'

'May I ask why?'

'Karim was working day and night on that Dubai deal. He really had his teeth in the bloody thing, you know? Said there was something that kept messing up his models and that he'd reported it to the CIO.'

'That's right,' I said and sat up. 'He told us when we all had dinner, didn't he. It'd been bothering him for a while. He first mentioned it when we met at the *Drum*, after his computer crashed and he freaked out.'

'I remember. You said as much.' The smile was audible in Djamal's voice, and I smiled, too.

'And you said you were familiar with his temper tantrums.'

'Allah, am I ever,' Djamal said. 'I never thought there were so many swearwords in the whole world and the galaxy. Fascinating, from a linguistic point of view. Did he tell you the marketing boss was all over him, too?'

'He didn't, no. Why, what happened?'

Something metallic clinked at the other line and I heard Djamal swear softly. Then he was back. 'Sorry about that,' he said. 'Dropped my pen. I don't know what happened, Karim never talked about work.

I mean, he talked about work pretty much all the time, but he never gave away details.'

'I know. That's what I told Gregson, too.'

'Did he believe you?'

'Let's just say he didn't sound convinced. What does the marketing boss have to do with Karim's calculations?'

'That's what Karim couldn't fathom, either. Said he had nothing to do with marketing ever, except when a new presentation template came out that he found crap. But the bloke must have showed up at his office a couple of times, asking all kinds of questions – how's the deal going, has he booked his flights yet, do the numbers look okay, were the investors happy, you know, small talk nonsense. Karim said that for a while he thought the guy was trying to chat him up, only he didn't show up on his gaydar.'

I rolled my eyes. Karim's gaydar. According to him, half his colleagues were gay. And the other half were in the closet.

'I don't know, John, but it doesn't look like the police are trying very hard.'

'Give them some time. This is not CSI. I guess real life investigations take longer than the TV shows try to make us believe.'

Chapter Twenty-Four

When I met with Karim's sister a few weeks later, the investigation hadn't progressed much. Hadn't progressed at all, to tell the truth.

'It looks as if the police just don't care about Karim's death,' Lina said, adjusting her sunglasses. 'That horrible policeman keeps saying it was a terrorist attack, and they're waiting to hear back from their terrorist expert group.'

'A terrorist attack?' I asked, incredulous. 'That's absurd. Terrorists would have blown the whole place up instead of putting one bullet into one person.'

She snivelled and rummaged around in her suitcase-sized handbag. I reached into the front pocket of my messenger bag and pushed a packet of tissues her way. She thanked me with a small smile and blew her nose, making elephant noises, just like her brother.

'But he was Muslim, and gay, John.'

'So? He was also a British citizen and a brilliant analyst at one of the hotshot banks around here. What if he was on to something fishy? The banks should know better by now, and, still, they're in the headlines with all kinds of crooked deals.'

'You think so?'

I shrugged. 'Dunno, but he kept mentioning he had stumbled across something he found strange,' and I told her everything I knew, including the bit about the marketing bloke.

'Should I talk to Maik about it? He's meeting the bank's head of legal for lunch on Monday. Maybe he can nudge someone.'

Maik was her husband, a highly successful business lawyer. I shook my head. 'That might be too much. I have another idea. Let me talk to someone else first.'

'No chance,' said that someone else that evening at Baker Street. 'Gregson's in full blocking mode, and there's no need to try and go through Lestrade. She's got a triple homicide on her hands, fascinating stuff. Interpol's trying to rip it out of her hands because somehow Belgium and France are involved, too. Want to see a real live fire-breathing dragon? Go watch Lestrade. Brilliant.'

He sighed. 'If only she'd ring me up. It's going a bit slow at the moment and I'm bloody bored.'

'Sherlock. Karim's murder, yeah? What of it?'

'Oh, that. Like I said, I tried needling Gregson, but he's as communicative as a brick. And about as clever, too. They've finally dropped the terrorist theory–'

I snorted. 'Yeah, I heard about that.'

'And from what I've read between the lines, the case is currently being treated as an unfortunate isolated incident.'

'What?'

'There's no CCTV footage, no-one's been seen coming and going other than the registered players, and the police already have their hands full.'

'I don't understand,' I said. 'Karim was next in line for a fat promotion and had just secured a huge deal. Don't you think his employer should send in their suit squad, ready to sue the laser tag company for insufficient security, rattling all kinds of sabres at the police? I mean, one of theirs was shot during a so-called team event. And they just shrug it off? Too bad, next?'

'That's all I was able to find out today. I'm sorry, John.'

'Fuck.' I slammed my hand on the table. 'I understand the police are understaffed and overworked and they don't follow up on each and every theft, but murder?'

'What makes you so sure it was anything other than an unfortunate incident?'

I stared at him. 'Sherlock, aren't you the brain, here? A single shot to the head? How is that unfortunate, other than for Karim?'

'Not the shooting as such, no, that was certainly planned. But what if Karim merely happened to be in the wrong spot at the wrong time?'

'What if he did stumble across something and was about to disclose it?'

Sherlock narrowed his eyes and worried his lower lip. 'Tell me again how he noticed, and what. He was working on a deal, you say?'

'Yes. He was going through his calculations when we spoke, and he said he hoped the irregularities were reflected in the agreement. And something messed up his models, like files sitting where they didn't belong.'

I frowned, trying to remember Karim's exact words. 'He said it looked as if someone was running a side business, or something like that. I'm sorry but I can't remember exactly.'

'What kind of deal was it? Do you know?'

'No, he never discussed the details of his work with anyone outside his team. Some tricky real estate transaction, I'd say. That was his specialty.'

'Do you have any names, colleagues he got along with, an office friend maybe?'

'There's Phoebe,' I said. 'I know he worked together closely with a Phoebe but I don't know her surname.'

He pulled up his laptop. 'What's the company's name?'

'Timmerton Group,' I said after a moment of thought. 'Yes, that's it. Timmerton. And they're on Fleet Street. No, Canary Wharf. They moved to Canary Wharf a while ago, I think.'

Sherlock entered the name into a search engine. 'Got it. Now let me see,' he mumbled, clicking his way through the website. 'About us; Who we are; no and no, oh, here: people.' He scrolled. 'Phoebe Henderson, Director.' He turned his laptop around. 'That her?'

I looked at the photo of a blonde woman. She didn't look familiar at all.

'Could be,' I said. 'I never actually met her. I only know she's a blonde with short hair so yeah, it's possible. Maybe Djamal knows her? He said Phoebe was the only one at work who knew about Karim and him.'

'Do you have his number?'

'I do, yes.'

'Good. I'll get in touch with him.' Sherlock closed the laptop and pulled his legs up to sit cross-legged. 'Tell me about Karim's work. What did he do? When did he usually get to work in the mornings? How did he get along with his managers? Was he involved in any rivalry games?'

'You mean pissing contests among his peers?'

'That sort of thing, yes. Try to remember all the details, everything he's ever told you.'

'Why would you want to know?'

'Just humour me, please.'

And so I dug down deep into my brain and told Sherlock everything I knew about Karim's job. His 80-hour weeks, his 24-7 availability for his customers and managers, his thrill whenever he'd reached another milestone, his business trips all over the world, how observing the Ramadan regularly got him into discussions with his manager because he cut down his working hours to 10 per day because fasting and relentless number crunching didn't work for him (I cast a meaningful glance at Sherlock when I mentioned that, but he didn't so much as blink), and that he routinely backed up his work twice a day because he didn't trust the company's IT infrastructure.

'Wait, what?' Sherlock uncrossed his legs. 'Do you know how he backed up his work?'

'Huh?'

'Memory sticks? Cloud? External hard drive?'

'I'm not sure. Back at uni, he used to save everything he worked on to a stick attached to his key ring. Don't know if he still does that. Did that, I mean.'

'It's a good place to start. Only, if a data stick was attached to his key ring, then chances are it's already been checked by the police during their initial investigation. They're frighteningly stupid at times but, alas, not that stupid. I'll think of something. In the meantime, will you let me distract you?'

I leaned back, distracted already.

'What did you have in mind?'

He slid out of his chair and came to kneel at my feet, placed his chin on my knee, and looked up at me with wide-eyed innocence.

'That depends on where you'd like to play. Around here, I'm thinking of something a little more one-sided, with me between your legs like this,' he nudged my knees apart and inched closer to where I felt my jeans become slightly uncomfortable, 'my hands sliding along your thighs like this,' he demonstrated, and I opened my legs a little wider, 'my fingers fumbling with your fly buttons like this…really John, one day I'd like to show you how swiftly I can open a zipper with my teeth, but you'd have to wear something other than your beloved Levi's.' *Pop* went the last button. 'Or at least a different model. Not that I'm complaining. You wear your 501s well.'

I looked down to where he teased along the waistband of my briefs with his long fingers. The fingers of his left hand, with which he pressed the violin strings. The fingers with the calloused tips. I shuddered and shifted in my seat, lifted my pelvis a little to offer myself to him. He smiled.

'You like my hands on your prick, don't you?'

'Mhm-hm.'

His smile deepened and he traced the outline of my hardening cock. 'So sexy when you're hot,' he murmured, pulled the fabric down, and bent forward to suck the tip between his lips.

I gasped.

'This is…ah, yes, like that. What other games were you thinking of? *Christ!* Not that I'm – careful there! – opposed to what you're doing now.'

He looked up into my face, his lips stretched around my length. He pulled back, inch by agonising inch, and let my prick fall against my stomach with a distinctly unsexy *plop*.

'The other option,' he said and wiped his lips, 'would be to take this to a bedroom, preferably yours because it's closer, and it would involve lube, a condom or no condom, both our hands and tongues, my arse, and your prick. What say you?'

'Bedroom. Quick, before I start wilting. I'm not exactly 25 anymore, you know.'

With a laugh, he reached for my hands and stood up. 'Don't be ridiculous, John. You're 37 and I've yet to see you fail to perform. Your bedroom it is.'

I let him haul me out of the armchair and reached for him but he wormed out of the way and fled to my bedroom. I followed him, half laughing, half cursing, trying to pull my T-shirt over my head and hold my jeans up at the same time.

Sherlock was shedding his lounge pants when I got there, let them fall to the floor and climbed onto the bed to kneel in the middle, legs spread, palming himself.

'Strip for me, John,' he said. 'Slowly. I want to watch you.'

His eyes were very dark, and his tongue darted out to wet his lips. I followed it with my eyes, then dropped my gaze to his hardening cock and felt mine respond in kind. I stopped fumbling with my shirt and reached for the hem to pull it up woman-style, with my arms crossed in front. I knew he liked to watch me undress, and I was comfortable enough in my skin to enjoy his eyes on me. And so I pulled my shirt up over my head, slowly, and pushed my jeans and briefs down, slowly, with Sherlock's eyes glued to my body, his hand pumping up and down along his length.

'Will you leave some of that for me?' I asked and pulled off my socks, giving his erection a pointed look. 'Or do you intend to make this a one-sided thing after all?'

I knelt down on the corner of my bed and crawled towards him on my hands and knees. Not that there was an awful long distance to crawl but I did crawl, making a show of it, my eyes not leaving Sherlock's face. He let go of his prick and scooted all the way back to the headboard, beckoning for me to come and get him, which I did. The devil in him challenged the devil in me, and I grabbed him around the waist and flipped him over on his stomach, using my heavier build to full advantage, and went straight for his pretty, firm arse. Sherlock was as neat and clean as a cat where his personal hygiene was concerned, and so I had no qualms when I pulled his cheeks apart. I licked and teased at his entrance until he started whimpering and lifted his hips with his legs spread wide, his sac hot and heavy and very inviting.

With a calm that belied the urgency that was building up inside me I nibbled along his perineum with my lips, licked his balls and sucked them into my mouth. The noises he produced made me want to reach for my cock, but that would have meant letting go of him, and that was out of the question. Too good was his begging, too sweet were his moans, and so I licked and nibbled my way back to his puckered hole and fucked inside with my tongue. Now, rimming is not for everyone, and I'll be the first to admit that it is a touchy subject for me, too. The slightest doubt about my partner's hygiene, and it's off the list. With Sherlock, however, I found I couldn't get enough of his arse. Pretty, tight, clean and oh, the sounds he made each time I dipped inside.

I can't say it often enough, but I loved having a partner who wasn't silent in bed. Moans and whimpering and begging were music to my ears, and Sherlock was beautifully shameless when it came to giving feedback.

When he let me know he was ready, or rather: demanded that I replace my tongue with my prick – 'now, John!' – I pulled him up and positioned myself behind him, sitting back on my heels. It was a position I'd always loved but hadn't tried since my knee replacement. But it had been a good leg week, and it was time to find out whether or not this position was to remain on the list of doable things, and so I guided him down to sit on my cock. He placed one hand against the wall to stabilise himself and looked over his shoulder, wild-eyed and with flushed cheeks.

'This is perfect,' he said huskily. 'I love how you fill me so completely.'

'You're beautiful, riding me like that.' I trailed my hand along his spine, feeling the bump of each vertebra. He shivered. 'I don't know if I should take it slow, or if I should fuck you hard.'

'Give me your cock. I love it when you pound into me. Fuck me hard, please, John.'

'As you wish.'

But when my thighs started burning, and my leg sent the first distress signals, I pushed Sherlock forward so he came to land on his hands and knees and gave him the pounding he had asked for, loving every single thrust and stroke, every moan, curse, hiss and word fragment, mine and his. My flesh slapped against his, making obscene and insanely hot noises, and the smell of sex, of Sherlock's lust and heat, filled my senses and made me go even harder until Sherlock stiffened below me and made an almost keening sound I'd never before heard him make, and then I felt him spasm around me, his inner muscles clenching and unclenching my cock until everything narrowed down to a tunnel of white heat through which I sped towards my release, grunting like a caveman and not caring a damn. And then…silence. Contentment. Peace.

No matter how sensitive a quality latex condom is, nothing will ever beat the sensation of shooting your load into your partner. I probably wouldn't say it out loud because it does sound a little primitive, doesn't it, 'shoot your load,' but that's what it is, rather

Neanderthal. You mark your sex partner as yours, but while Sherlock let me dominate him in bed I knew damn well it was his choosing. It was exactly like he had said: he loved it when I pounded into him. I think it grounded him in a way, got him out of his head and back into his body, and I was fine with that. More than fine: it thrilled and delighted me that he wanted me so much.

So yes, having unprotected sex with Sherlock Holmes was a thing of beauty.

The ensuing dribbling of my semen out of him and onto my sheets, not so much, but when I remarked on it, he laughed and shrugged.

'My bed next time,' he said. 'Feeling you like that is worth a little discomfort.'

He yawned and turned to lie on his stomach. 'Good night, John.'

Point made.

CHAPTER TWENTY-FIVE

'WHY HAVE YOU SUITED UP LIKE THAT?' I LOOKED SHERLOCK UP AND DOWN. 'Lunch with Mycroft again?'

'No,' Sherlock replied, adjusting his cufflinks. 'The Timmerton Group has a pre-audit scheduled, starting next week. Today, they are expecting an advance visit by one Neil O'Donahue who will assess the status of the company's documentation and report back to the audit team. How do I look?'

He straightened lapels that didn't need straightening and turned to me with an expectant look in his eyes.

'You look like something I want to peel out of its tailored shell and eat for breakfast,' I promptly said, and he laughed.

'You are a sex fiend, John. I shudder to think what you were like in your early 20s.'

'Younger. Both knees. Less grey in my hair.'

'Ah, but your greying temples are sexy.' He pressed a quick kiss to my forehead. 'Seriously, John, do I look like an auditor?'

'I don't know many auditors,' I said. 'But you look like you're about to audition for that law show you like to watch.'

And he did. Sherlock looked tall, sleek and smooth in his dark grey three-piece, discreetly patterned tie and pocket square. His shoes were polished to shine, his hair was combed into obedience, and a pair of dark-rimmed glasses completed the picture.

'Mycroft would be proud of you,' I added, grinning.

He nodded and reached for a slim, expensive-looking leather case.

'I'll stop over at the Met before I come home,' he said. 'Lestrade got stuck in her international case and has asked me for input. And I want to go through Karim's file. I need to find out whether there was a memory stick somewhere amongst his belongings.'

'I won't be home before six or seven. Tim has the week off and we're taking over most of his patients.'

'Got it. See you tonight then.'

'See you tonight, Sherlock. Be safe. And don't do anything stupid, Mr O'Donahue.'

'Don't worry your pretty head, darrrling,' he said with a wink and an exaggerated burr. 'I've done this before.'

'Do I want to know?'

'Nope,' he said and laughed. Another quick kiss, this one to my lips, and Neil O'Donahue was out the door.

SOMETIME THAT AFTERNOON I got a text from Sherlock telling me no memory stick had been found, or had been reported and whether I could arrange for him to look through Karim's flat.

I'll have to check with his sister, I texted back. *Will let you know.*

There were a few more minutes before open surgery started, and so I rang Lina.

'The police have already been through Karim's flat,' she said. 'What does your friend hope to achieve?'

'He has a knack for seeing things others don't. Please, Lina? I give you my word he will not damage anything. I'll be there, too.'

'I know that. It's just that I...oh, why not. A fresh set of eyes can't hurt. Let me check something.' I heard a rustling sound and some clicking, then she was back. 'Maik is taking the girls to see Mateesha tonight. I could move my training session forward and meet you if it's not too short notice for you.'

'Who is Mateesha?'

'Who is Mateesha? Seriously, John?' I could see her roll her dark eyes. 'If I didn't know you don't have teenage children, you'd have given yourself away now. Mateesha is the current reigning diva.'

'Oh.'

'That's what Maik said, too.'

'And yet he goes.'

'Daddy time for his girls.'

'Good man.'

'*Mashallah*. So, will tonight work for you?'

'Can't see why not.' I didn't need to cross-check anything because my evenings were rarely booked, and I hoped Sherlock hadn't scheduled anything for tonight, either. 'When?'

'How about eight?'

'That'll work. Thank you, Lina. See you tonight.'

'See you, John.'

We rang off and I sent a short text to Sherlock.

> Karim's place tonight at 8. Can you make it?
> *Yes. My arse hurts btw.*
> Careful what you wish for.
> *That wasn't a complaint.*
> Noted.
> *Can I have some more?*
> Not now. I'm about to see my next patient.
> *Wouldn't you rather see me?*
> Down, boy.
> *Down you or down me?*
> Quiet.

And I put my phone away before this conversation got out of hand. A suspected tonsillitis was next, and I couldn't afford to let anything distract me from a seven-year-old in pain.

'KARIM'S OFFICE HAS ALREADY been cleared out,' Sherlock said while I was going through the refrigerator.

A plastic bowl with what looked like larvae sat next to the butter and I binned both without asking.

'How do you know that?' Luckily eggs came with a sealed shell, and the tinned mushrooms and tomatoes were unharmed, too.

'Because that was the office Neil O'Donahue was given to go through the first batch of documents.'

'What a coincidence.'

'Wasn't it.'

'I take it his computer was gone, too?'

'Oh, there was a computer all right. Brand new and shiny, waiting to be used by the lucky soul taking over this lovely corner office.'

'Did you meet Phoebe?'

'I did indeed. Are you making an omelette?'

Sherlock had come to stand behind me and peered over my shoulder.

'That's the idea. Why, interested?'

'I wouldn't mind trying.'

'I thought you never eat while you're working. Sharpens the brain and all that.'

'A nibble won't hurt.'

'Since when?'

He nibbled the side of my neck and I shivered.

'Nibbling is good,' he said with a grin, put his chin on my shoulder, and wrapped his arms loosely around my waist. 'Phoebe took a while to warm up to good old Neil, but before she left for her next meeting she pointed out a section in the company's HR files and guess what.'

'Mhm?'

'For each employee from director onwards, there's a bank-owned life insurance.'

'Meaning what?'

'If I understood the paperwork correctly, it's basically to cover the cost of employees' benefits, a fairly standard thing to have. However, if the employee dies, it's the company that receives the insurance sum, not the family.'

Anger flared up inside of me, and I turned to look at Sherlock.

'Are you implying that Karim was shot so the company could cash in an insurance check?'

He gave a one-sided shrug. 'I need to have somebody else look at this and tell me for sure. I'm not an expert.'

'Please don't tell me there's something you don't know,' I said, trying for a lighter tone. Working myself into a rage over something that had only just appeared on the far end of the list of possibilities wasn't going to help.

'There's lots of things I don't know.' He nuzzled the curve of my neck, unglued himself from me and heaved himself up to sit on the kitchen counter. 'I don't know how to chop veggies as quickly as you can.'

'I'm a trained surgeon. I'm good with knives. Onion.'

'What?'

'Hand me the onion, please. Thank you. Now watch me chop.'

'Will you cry?'

'Probably. That's what onions do. They make people cry.'

And I chopped. And I snivelled, with the onion only partially to blame. But the omelette was good, and Sherlock did more than nibble. Good thing there were some leftovers in the freezer.

LINA MET US OUTSIDE the apartment building. She greeted me with a smile and held her hand out to Sherlock.

'You must be John's friend,' she said. 'I'm Lina Nair, Karim's sister.'

'Sherlock Holmes.' Sherlock took the offered hand. 'I'm very sorry for your loss.'

'Thank you. Are you with the police?'

'I am not. I do occasionally assist them as an external consultant, but today I am here solely as John's friend.'

She typed in the security code, and we followed her inside. 'And what if you find something?'

'In that case, I'll speak to my main contact at the Met.'

'Please tell me it's not that horrible policeman I've had to deal with all the time. He didn't seem very trustworthy.'

'He's too stupid to be untrustworthy,' Sherlock said dismissively. 'If my contact can't help either, well, then I have another ace up my sleeve.'

He met her dubious glance with one of his boyish grins. Lina's left eyebrow shot up to meet her hijab but she returned his grin with a smile of her own.

Karim's flat was on the eighth floor, and we rode up in silence. Lina was fiddling with the tassel of her handbag, Sherlock was studying the security note on the opposite wall, and I stared at the floor, trying to remember the last time I'd been here.

Isn't it strange how it's always in retrospect that you realise how much time you lose doing things that hold little to no importance, instead of spending it with people who mean so much to you? How often had we postponed and cancelled our pub nights and gaming sessions or had not been to the rugby matches we had planned to see because something had come up, either on his side or on mine?

The lift doors opened, calling me back into reality, and we followed Lina to the door of Karim's flat.

'Like I said, the police have already gone through his things,' she said, fishing for his coded keycard in her purse. She pushed the door open. 'They had his computer checked– *Allah!*'

'What is it?'

CHAPTER TWENTY-SIX

SHE PUSHED THE DOOR FURTHER TO REVEAL WHAT HAD BEEN KARIM'S tastefully furnished bachelor's den. A stream of angry Arabic left her mouth, and I thought I recognised some of the words, none of which would have been fit for her teenage daughters to hear.

The place was a mess. Books, CDs, and DVDs lay opened amidst newspaper clippings, most of them torn and broken in two, a bookshelf had been torn down, the colourful sofa cushions had been cut open and the drawers of Karim's antique bureau stood open with half their contents spilt on the floor.

'Ten thousand djinn upon them,' Lina shrieked, sounding like a djinn herself. 'Will you look at that!' She dropped to her knees, reached for a leather-bound volume from which a good third of its pages had been torn and now lay scattered on the floor.

'They defiled his Quran, the filthy dogs.' She clutched the book to her chest and started crying. 'It was our father's, who gave it to Karim when he passed his exams. He was so proud of his youngest.'

Sherlock opened his mouth as if to say something, but I touched his arm, stopping him with a look. Now was not a good time to say anything, and I quickly closed the door, hoping we hadn't attracted unwanted attention. Unlike their older brother, the younger Halabis were emotional firebrands. Once ignited, it was best to wait until the storm had died down, and I signalled for Sherlock to follow me into Karim's office.

'Well well,' Sherlock said, peering into the chaos that used to be Karim's pristine little work cell. 'It looks as though your theory wasn't that far-fetched after all. He may well have stumbled across something.'

'On a scale from one to delusional, how would you rate your chance of finding something here?'

'That would depend on the wager.'

I looked over my shoulder to make sure Lina was not within hearing range, brought my lips close to his ear and whispered, 'You think your arse hurts now?'

His cheeks turned pink and he grinned. 'Challenge accepted.'

And he sat down cross-legged on the floor with his back to the door, taking in the scenery. I knew better than to wait for an immediate response when he slipped into this strange insta-trance of his, and so I went back into the living room where Lina was still kneeling on the floor with Karim's Quran cradled in her arms. She was no longer crying but her eyes held the look of a wounded animal.

'This wasn't the police, right?' she asked.

I shook my head. 'I don't think so.' I crouched down carefully. 'Lina, can you think of anything at all that may be of interest to Sherlock, if not the police? Minor stuff even.'

'Nothing at all. Believe me, John, I've been thinking of hardly anything else, but there was nothing different at all, not to my knowledge. I mean, I wasn't exactly familiar with his daily rituals. I can't tell you at what time he usually got up or whether he showered in the morning or in the evening.'

'Evening,' I said without thinking. 'He liked to wash the day's dirt off before he went to bed.'

'See?' Her eyes filled with tears again, and she angrily wiped them away. How she managed that without smearing her kohl and mascara, I had no idea. The secrets of make-up were forever lost on me.

'You know more about him than I did.' She dug in her purse and produced what looked like another headscarf. 'My back-up,' she explained. 'There's a sad number of people who take offence at seeing a Muslim woman wear her *hijab*.'

I looked at her, stunned. 'People really do that?'

'You'd be surprised how low people can sink when they think they're right. That's why Maik hired a driver-slash-bodyguard for me.'

She carefully wrapped the Quran in the scarf and placed it into her purse, then started as if to clean up the mess.

'I don't think we should be doing that,' I said. 'We should call the police. It is a crime scene, after all.'

'You think so?'

'I'm afraid so. Let me check with Sherlock as soon as he is done in Karim's office. He knows better about police procedures than I do.'

I stood up and offered her my hand to help her up. She accepted and gracefully rose from her kneeling position.

'What is it your friend does for a living? A police consultant, he said? What does that entail?'

'He's a bit like a posh private detective, working for the Met on a fairly regular basis. I think – and don't quote me on this – it's not only to take some of the stress off the chronically understaffed teams, but also because Sherlock can go places and do things a sworn-in officer of the law cannot go or do.'

'That's quite correct, John,' Sherlock said from behind. 'I do their sneak work for them. And then some.'

He walked over to the wall where Karim had hung a number of photos. Most of them had been torn down but a few were still in their spots. 'There's the two of you,' he said with amusement in his voice. 'You look really young in these photos.'

He had to be looking at the rugby photos.

'In my early 20s, Sherlock,' I said and his head snapped around, but he didn't say anything and focussed on another, more recent one.

'When was this taken? You look more like yourself in that one.'

I came to stand next to him. He had picked up a photo in a broken frame that showed Karim and me before the mother of all fairytale castles, Neuschwanstein in Bavaria, Germany.

'About two years ago,' I said and touched my hand to Karim's smiling face. 'He dragged me to bloody Oktoberfest, and we did a quick scenic tour afterwards. He didn't drink alcohol,' I hastened to assure Lina who nodded.

'I know that. Karim was a faithful man.' She took the photo from Sherlock's hand and gave it to me. 'Crime scene or not, this is yours,' she said. 'Please. I insist. You both look so happy in it.'

'Thank you.' I cradled the framed photo to my chest, just as she had cradled the Quran. 'We had fun in Bavaria.'

Sherlock, in the meantime, had turned his attention to the living room. 'A memory stick,' he murmured. 'Something tells me it's not been found.'

'What makes you so sure?' Lina asked.

'Look at the state of his flat,' Sherlock replied. 'I'm surprised they haven't torn down the walls. Doesn't look like the site of a successful bounty hunt to me.'

He wandered around the room, careful not to step on anything. 'That the bedroom over there?' He pointed and I nodded.

The bedroom looked a little better than the living room, probably because there wasn't too much to be torn off the walls, with the exception of a framed *Star Wars* print depicting Karim's favourite princess, who was staring up at us from behind broken glass, blaster pointed at us.

'How dare they,' Sherlock muttered. 'She is royalty.' He knelt down to look under the bed. 'Nothing. Guess it would have been too–

'What have we here?' He gave a low whistle as something on the floor by the wardrobe caught his attention.

'What?' Lina and I asked, at the same time.

He stepped over two piles of clothing to pick something up.

'I think this is the droid I'm looking for,' he said with a grin and held up a white-and-blue droid figurine. 'Help me, little friend, you're my only hope.'

'But that's...isn't that too small to hold a memory stick?'

'Really, John, you should know better. The Death Star plans weren't on a memory stick.' He held the figurine up and inspected it from all angles. 'They were on a – aha!' He carefully removed the droid's supporting leg.

'Mrs Nair, do you happen to have a pair of tweezers in that very fashionable handbag of yours?'

'I most certainly do.' She produced a slim case, opened it, and took out the requested item. 'Careful, please,' she said. 'I use it on my eyebrows.'

'Don't worry. I won't need to apply brute force.' And he didn't. 'Behold,' Sherlock said with a triumphant grin. 'The missing piece.'

I squinted at the tiny thing he held up with the tweezers. 'Is that a SIM card?'

'It's a micro SD card,' Sherlock corrected and handed the tweezers back to Lina. 'Oh, Karim was a clever one.'

'How come you found this within minutes without touching anything?' Lina asked, putting the tweezers back. 'I don't understand.'

'It may be hard to believe, but there are those who have never heard of a galaxy far, far away. For those heathens, this little fellow here,' he held the figurine up, 'is nothing but a useless toy to collect dust in a grown man's bedroom. But once you realise that particular grown man was a firm believer in said galaxy, the only question you have to ask yourself is: *What would Princess Leia do?*'

He pulled out his wallet and placed the micro card into one of the slots on the inside. 'I am done for now,' he said. 'I think it's time to call the police and report the break-in.'

DI GREGSON AND A team of three arrived about half an hour later.

'Holmes,' he said after greeting Lina. 'What on earth do you think you're doing here?'

'Mr Holmes is here in his capacity as consulting investigator,' Lina said.

'To do what?'

'To look into the circumstances of my brother's death.'

'The police are already investigating the case.'

'Surely a fresh set of eyes won't hurt, Inspector,' she said with a sweet smile. 'And I did call the police when I saw the flat had been broken into.'

'We haven't touched anything, Gregson,' Sherlock added, just as sweetly. 'The crime scene has not been compromised.'

'I should hope not.' Gregson nodded to his team. 'Get going.'

'Would you like my assistance?'

'Thanks, but no thanks, Holmes. We are quite capable of assessing the scene of a break-in without you prancing about. Unless your...client insists?'

'I am sure Mr Holmes has seen all he needs to see,' Lina said. 'Mr Holmes, John, thank you for agreeing to meet me here, but I believe there is nothing we can hope to achieve tonight. With your permission, I should like to place the break-in into the capable hands of Inspector Gregson. May I see you tomorrow to discuss the next steps, Mr Holmes?'

'Certainly, Mrs Nair,' Sherlock replied. 'Thank you for placing your trust in me.'

'You're John's friend,' Lina smiled at him, then me. 'He trusts you. How could I not?'

'Does your husband know about this?' Gregson cut in.

'About what?'

'About you hiring Holmes.'

'Not yet. Why is that of any interest? Karim was my brother, not my husband's.'

'I just thought–' he broke off and looked to the floor, probably realising he'd been about to say something inappropriate.

'You thought I needed my husband's permission before making

a decision?' There was poison mixed into the sweetness of her voice. 'How very traditional, Inspector Gregson. My money is mine to spend, and my husband has better things to do with his time than to do my thinking for me.'

She checked the time on her elegant wristwatch. 'Dear me, how time flies. I'm afraid I have to go. Unless I'm needed at the crime scene, Inspector?'

'That won't be necessary, Mrs Nair,' Gregson hastily assured her.

'I didn't think so.' Lina took a business card from her purse and handed it to Gregson. 'I am sure you have it all on file but here are my contact details, just in case. Good evening, Inspector.'

'Good evening, Mrs Nair.' He gave us the briefest of nods. 'Holmes. Watson.'

'YOU KNOW, YOU COULD report him for what he said,' Sherlock said when Lina's car pulled up. A young woman in a dark tailored suit got out to open the passenger door for her.

Lina shrugged. 'He's not worth wasting my time and energy on.' She handed her handbag to the young woman. 'Thank you, Sofia.' Before she climbed in, she turned to Sherlock. 'Will you accept this case? Officially, I mean?'

'I would be glad to, Mrs Nair,' Sherlock said.

She smiled at him and held out her hand. 'I like what I've seen so far. Please call me Lina.'

'Thank you, Lina,' Sherlock replied and took her hand. 'I promise I will do all that I can do to find out what happened to your brother. Please call me when it's convenient for you, and we'll discuss the details.'

'I will.'

They exchanged business cards, then she got into the car, and we watched as the sleek limousine pulled off.

'I like her,' Sherlock said. 'Is she anything like her brother?'

'She is. They have the same eyes and the same tendency to swear in Arabic. She's more elegant than he was, but they both have a head for numbers. Karim was an investment animal, and Lina is working as a tax advisor.'

I chuckled. 'God help Gregson if he ever decides to truly insult her. She'll snap her fingers and her husband will bring in a horde of blood-thirsty suits in defence of his wife.'

'Do give Lestrade a heads-up if this ever comes to pass so she can book a front row seat.'

I laughed. 'Too bad she isn't the one handling the case.'

'Too bad indeed.' Sherlock cleared his throat. 'Now, that wager you mentioned–'

I raised my arm to hail an on-coming cab.

CHAPTER TWENTY-SEVEN

FOR THE NEXT COUPLE OF DAYS I WAS LIVING WITH A GHOST. OH, I STILL SAW Sherlock, but it was more like sightings of him. He scurried by, mumbling to himself. He didn't get out of his pyjamas, didn't speak, didn't listen, didn't eat or drink. At least not when I was within sight or earshot. Before I left for work in the mornings, I left sandwiches, water, and a Thermos on the kitchen table, much like offerings for a leprechaun, and it was all gone when I got home, which I considered a small victory.

'Are you getting somewhere?' I ventured to ask him when we happened to be in the living room at the same time.

He looked up from his laptops – yes, plural, as there were three arranged on the coffee table, all of which he operated via a weird-shaped keyboard and a clunky mouse – and blinked as his eyes focussed on me.

'Mhm?'

'I said, are you getting somewhere?'

'I am, yes. Karim was a very clever one indeed.'

'Why is that?'

'The card held a complete back-up of all of his work-related files, all of his calculations and models, plus all source files needed to ensure the links and short-cuts are functioning outside the company network.'

'And that is good?'

'Oh, it's very good. It took me a while to crack it all because it's been heavily encrypted, in case the card was to fall into the wrong hands.'

'Yours.'

'No. I am not the enemy here.'

'Who is, then?'

'His employer is.'

'What?'

'I believe that in his efforts to prepare the best and most flawless model for the complex transaction he was working on, Karim has opened the proverbial box of Pandora simply by cross-referencing his worst-case assumptions.'

'Huh?'

'He found the groundwork for a deal he was not supposed to know about.'

'What was it?'

'That's what I'm trying to find out.'

'And that's all on the card we found?' I sat down.

'His work, yes. All of his figures and notes. Brilliant stuff, brilliant. Flawlessly linked, very complex formulas. I love it. The rest, no. I need access to the company network, and you can imagine how far I've got there.'

'I suppose they have good firewalls.'

'You suppose right. Ha!' His face lit up and he began to type. 'There,' he said, satisfied. 'I thought that'd be of interest.'

'What is it?'

'Just because I don't know how to get past the firewalls doesn't mean nobody else does.'

'Ah,' I said. 'You know people who do stuff. Right?'

'Exactly right. Well done, John.'

'Are you making fun of me?'

'Not at all. I'm glad you're paying attention to what I tell you.'

I huffed. 'I'm not all stupid, you know.'

'Of course you're not,' he said, disapproval in his voice. 'You're a bit slow sometimes, but you've earned a medical degree from a renowned university. Can't be stupid for that.'

'Thanks. I feel a lot better now.'

'You're welcome. Besides, I don't fuck stupid people.'

'Hear, hear.'

'I'm serious, John. I can't bear stupid. You're a man of medicine, not a math genius. There's no shame in not being brilliant in all fields.'

'This is getting better and better. Next, you'll remind me how far we've progressed since the time we barber surgeons had to stay outside the city walls.'

He grinned. 'Now that you're bringing it up– Don't throw that, John. This equipment was not exactly cheap.'

'You're a shit, Sherlock, and you know it.'

'But a sexy shit, yes?'

'Not right now, you're not.'

'What would you do if– Oh, hello there,' he interrupted himself and smiled at the computer screen. 'I knew you'd take the bait. All set for tonight. Scalpel's on it. Now I need to eat. And I want to fuck.'

'What you want is a shower. And a shave. You look like something that's just crawled out from underneath a rock.'

He scratched his stubbled chin. 'It's not that bad, is it?'

'Shower,' I sternly said. 'And a shave. Or else no sex.'

He muttered something that held many sibilants.

'No need to seek refuge in speaking snake, Potter. Off to the bathroom.' I leaned back, grinning, as he shut down and unplugged his laptops, still muttering, but a tell-tale twitch in the corners of his mouth gave him away.

'And who on earth is Scalpel?'

'I'm not at liberty to say, my dear Watson.' Sherlock stood up and straightened his rumpled sleep-shirt with as much dignity as he could muster. 'Suffice to say they know how to cut their way through walls thought safe.'

'They?'

'As in, non-binary. They refuse to bend to the laws of heteronormativity.'

'I see. Now, shower. Or else–'

'How can you still look at yourself in the mirror, bullying me about like that?'

'Want me to ring up Mycroft so you can tell him all about your abusive flatmate?'

'God, no. Having my brother swoop down on me with his claws outstretched is the last thing I need.'

'Well then.'

SHERLOCK'S PHONE WENT OFF while he was in the shower. I checked the display, and, when I saw it was *G Lestrade* calling, I went to knock on the bathroom door.

'What?'

'Lestrade's calling.'

'What?'

The door was yanked open, and Sherlock stood before me in all of his naked glory, clean-shaven, his skin still damp, and his hair towelled half dry. He smelled good, and he looked delicious. Something in my face must have pleased him because he grinned.

'Like what you see?'

'Is that a trick question?'

'Give me my phone. Please.'

'It's on the sideboard where you left it.'

'If you want to look at my arse, all you have to do is ask. No need to make me parade back and forth.'

'Would you do that? Parade for me?'

'You, John Watson, are a perv.'

'And you, Sherlock Holmes, like the idea of parading for me.' I gave his groin a pointed look.

He looked down to where his cock was already at half height, signalling its agreement. 'It's got to be your officer's voice.'

'So you do have a military kink.'

'I like a man who knows what he wants.'

'In that case, I want you to ring Lestrade. And make it quick, soldier.'

'Sir, yes, sir!' He touched two fingers to his forehead in a mock salute and sauntered over to where his phone was lying, picked it up and dialled Lestrade's number. When the call connected, he turned around and leaned against the sideboard, putting himself on full display.

'Evening, Lestrade,' he said. 'What is it?' He listened intently, lazily stroking himself, his eyes holding mine.

'Are you sure about that? – I see. Well, that explains it. – What, now?' His eyes widened. 'Uh, yeah, I guess. – Twenty minutes?'

I held up my thumbs.

'Twenty minutes is fine. – Yes, all good. – Yes, John is here, too. – That would be just splendid. See you.'

He rang off, opened the top drawer, and threw me the lube.

'Hurry,' he said. 'We've got 20 minutes.'

'At ease.' I stuffed the bottle into my back pocket and walked up to him. 'Come here.'

I kissed him, and he melted against me, his lips warm and sweet on mine, but, sadly, 20 minutes was all we had, and so I pulled away from him, trailed my fingertips from the hollow of his throat down to his navel, then closed my hand around his erection. He made a small, needy sound.

'Let me take the edge off first,' I murmured against his skin and sank to my knees.

I loved sucking him off, and I did so with relish until he made that noise I loved hearing the most, that half-sobbing, half-whimpering sound that erupted from his throat just before he came. I knew he hated it, saying it made him sound as if he was begging, but I loved it because it told me I'd done well, and so I swallowed all he gave and licked him clean until he squirmed away.

I got up to my feet and jerked my chin towards the drawer. 'Condom,' I commanded.

He frowned. 'But we – oh. Of course.'

Being safe was all good, and having unprotected sex was great, but unprotected sex meant dribbling, and we had – I looked over at the old-fashioned clock on the wall – some 11 minutes left. I'd taken my sweet time with him, given our restricted time budget, and there was no time for thorough cleaning up.

'Good boy,' I said and took the condom from him. 'Now bend over and spread. Yeah, just like that. Christ, Sherlock, do you have any idea how fucking hot you are?'

He looked up and over his shoulder. 'Tick-tock.'

I unbuttoned, untucked, got sheathed, and lubed up. 'Does Lestrade have a key to this place?'

'Not yet – *ah!*' He hung his head and clenched his fists when my cock breached him.

'Then what's another minute?'

We were still at that stage where we humped each other whenever we could – minus the past few days – and Sherlock's beautifully responsive body welcomed me like the old friend I hoped to become. I slid inside without much effort, paused to give him time, kissed his shoulder blades and the sensitive area between them, which made him shiver and sigh, and bit the nape of his neck. Only when he signalled me he was good to go did I start thrusting. I would have preferred to go slower, to thoroughly enjoy him, but I'd do that as soon as Lestrade was gone.

It was over too quickly, too hot was the arse I was pounding into, too lust-crazed my mind, too sweet the noises Sherlock made.

I reached for his hands when I came, twined our fingers together and spilled, pressed my forehead between his shoulder-blades, breathing heavily, before I carefully, slowly pulled out of him.

'See? A condom was a good idea.' I pulled the thing off, tied a neat little knot, and reached for the tissue box. 'Nothing a quick wipe can't fix.' I sniffed. 'Maybe open the windows, just in case.'

Sherlock turned around as I got myself back in order.

'Hand me the tissues,' he said with a sheepish smile.

'Huh?'

'Tissues, please.' He gestured to where he had stood, bent over, and grinned. 'I'm afraid there was a small accident.'

'The hell, Sherlock?'

There was indeed evidence of a small accident, and it was dripping off the drawer handles.

'Where did that come from? Didn't you shoot down my throat only a few minutes ago?'

'I did.' He took the tissues from me and wiped his come off the sideboard. 'You're a great fuck. Best cock I've ever had.'

I snorted. 'You sure know how to make a boy blush.'

'You're no boy,' Sherlock stated matter-of-factly. 'And am I glad about that.'

'Thank you.'

'You're welcome.' He checked the time. 'I better get dressed.'

'Please do. We don't want to make Lestrade blush, too.'

Now he snorted. 'Don't be absurd, John. She's a grown-up woman. Besides, she's already seen me like this.'

'Seriously?'

'Sadly, yes. And considerably less well fed, too. Oh, don't fret,' he said dismissively. 'There is no danger of that anymore.'

'Of what?'

'Tick-tock,' he said and ran upstairs to get dressed.

The doorbell rang just as I pulled a fresh shirt over my head. I went to open the door, and Lestrade came up the stairs with two plastic bags in one hand and a lidded paper cup in the other.

'I took the liberty of bringing something to eat,' she said. 'Hello, Dr Watson. I hope you like Indian food.'

'I do, thank you. Hello, Inspector.'

She stepped inside and looked around. 'This looks very homey for a flat-share,' she observed. 'Last time I was here it was still a bit unorganised.'

'Last time – oh. The night you schlepped Sherlock home. It's been a while since then.'

'I take it you're the house elf around here, yes?'

'Give me a sock and I'm gone.'

She laughed. 'Where do I put this?' she asked, holding up the bags. 'Dumping the boxes on the table is probably no longer an option.'

'John likes to bring out our best linen when there's guests around,' Sherlock said, coming down his chicken-ladder. 'Evening, Lestrade.'

'Evening, Sherlock.'

He looked very dapper in a striped shirt, jeans rolled up at the ankles, and a pair of simple loafers on his feet, his hair neatly combed for once, and his eyes bright and alert. He looked freshly fucked, too, although I hoped Lestrade wouldn't notice that particular detail. But she cast me a sideways glance, the corners of her eyes crinkled, and I knew she knew.

'Let me take this.' I took the bags from her. 'I'll go polish the silver and prepare a tray.'

'See? All he needs is livery.'

'Do you need help with that, Dr Watson?'

'John, please,' I said. 'Call me John. And no, I'll be fine. I'm sure you have things to discuss with my charming flatmate, Inspector.'

'Gwen,' Lestrade said, holding out her hand.

I shifted the bags to one hand and we shook.

'Aww, now isn't that sweet.' Sherlock was watching us with raised eyebrows. 'You two bonded awfully quickly.'

'It's the pain we share over you that fuses us together. Wait, John, that's my Chai latte. That doesn't go anywhere. I didn't think to bring any for you, sorry about that.'

'No worries,' Sherlock sat down in his armchair, slipped out of his shoes and pulled up his legs. 'I already had some.'

Lestrade looked him over. 'Yes, I see that,' she said dryly.

I coughed and Sherlock grinned, not in the least embarrassed.

'Congratulations, Detective Inspector. I see you're beginning to pay attention to detail. Now, what brings you here?'

I went into the kitchen to distribute the food into bowls, got plates, forks and spoons and arranged everything on a tray. Any butler would have approved, I am sure. Before I went to feed the humans, I sliced up some cucumber and tomato for Bodie and Doyle. It was their dinner time, too.

'Are those yours, John? Or are you pig-sitting for somebody's kid?' Lestrade asked.

'They're mine now,' I said and placed the tray on the coffee table. 'They used to be my nieces'. Sherlock, put the computers away, please, so we can eat.'

He grumbled but uncrossed his legs and slid out of the chair to move his equipment from the table to a corner of the couch.

'My boys had guinea pigs, too, when they were little. Now we're discussing a dog. I'm not too wild about the idea, but I'm afraid it's three against one.'

'You have three sons?'

'Two sons and a husband. It's got to be a man thing, dogs, man's best friend and all.'

'Visions of Wellies, waxed coats, and vast green meadows, you mean?'

She chuckled, took the plates from the tray and placed them on the now empty table. Mostly empty, anyway.

'Something like that, I'm sure.'

'Send them to Wales. I can recommend a few B&Bs where your boys will find just that. And that includes the grown-up boy.'

'You're from Wales?'

'What gave it away?'

'*What gav' it away,*' she repeated. 'Softer vowels, maybe, and a bit of a sing-song. Your voice, most of all. You have one of those great Welsh voices, you know, like Sir Richard Burton or Sir Anthony Hopkins.'

'Oh wow, thank you. I've never been compared to Sir Richard before. That's very flattering.'

'You two want me to leave you alone?' Sherlock reached for one of the bowls and started filling up his plate. 'I can eat upstairs if you want to chit-chat.'

'I am awfully sorry for taking the spotlight away from you. I just realised that I never really spoke to John.'

'Is he helping with your cases?'

'No.'

'So why would you want to speak to him?'

'Because he's taken the main burden of looking after you off my shoulders, that's why.'

'Oh come *on*, Lestrade.'

She silenced him with a look, and my respect for her skyrocketed.

'How about we meet in a pub some time,' I suggested. 'Just us adults.'

'I would like that. We could compare notes.' She heaped a generous portion of chicken tikka on her plate. 'But I didn't actually come here to chit-chat. Nor did I come here to discuss the Zvianski case with you, sorry about that, Sherlock. That one's as good as closed.'

'But why did you ask about the missing moonstone?'

'Because that's something I've not been able to figure out. It's been gnawing at me, but all in all we're pretty much done.' She chewed thoughtfully. 'But just so we're clear, lads, the conversation we're about to have will never have taken place.'

'Understood,' I said, and Sherlock nodded his agreement, his mouth full.

'It would seem that your friend's murder is expected to end up on the cold case shelf, not to be touched again for a time period yet to be defined.'

I lowered my fork. 'What?'

'Solving the murder of Karim Halabi is not what the top ranks want us to do.'

'Why the hell not?' I asked, and Sherlock, at the same time: 'How did you find out?'

'I overheard Gregson being accused of not following the leads he's been given. A very fierce woman was doing a very fine job of taking him apart, probably the wife or a sister–'

'Sister,' I said. 'Karim had no wife. That would have been Lina Nair, his older sister.'

'A remarkable woman. Gregson looked like a schoolboy who hasn't done his homework.'

'That's his default setting.'

'Quiet, Sherlock. I know you and Gregson don't get along well, but while he may have a few faults–'

Sherlock made a derisive noise.

'–while he may have a few faults,' she repeated, 'he isn't lazy, and he doesn't neglect his duties. He's a very capable policeman–'

'Meaning, he is as inspiring as a slice of stale bread.'

'Will you be quiet, Holmes,' Lestrade snapped, and Sherlock lowered his eyes after a brief staring contest.

'As I was saying, Gregson may be many things but negligent he is not. On the contrary, what he lacks in creativity or intuition, he makes up for in diligence and doggedness. He will follow each and every lead and will sit and brood over his notes long after most of us have left.'

She reached for her tea and took a sip. 'So, hearing him being accused of not doing his job got me curious, and as soon as there was a chance I asked him what that had been about. Well, and from what I gather, he's had his instructions to postpone, delay, and stall for as long as possible.'

'Until a more pressing case would come up and the regrettable incident has to be handed over to a more inexperienced team without the necessary clearance to do some actual snooping around.' Sherlock pursed his lips. 'Mhm. Did Gregson mention any names?'

'He said his instructions came from the super, sorry, superintendent himself.'

'Willingsham, eh.'

'The very same,' she confirmed.

He sat his plate down. 'Will you give me my computer, John? No, not that one. The one with the apple on it. Yes. Thank you.' He opened it and after some scrolling and clicking uttered a triumphant 'Ha!', closed the laptop, and got up to retrieve his phone. 'Please excuse me,' he said, remembering his manners. 'I must make a quick phone call.'

Quick-dialling a number, he went to the kitchen. The call connected, and he started speaking in rapid Chinese.

'Who on earth is he talking to?'

Lestrade cocked her head and listened. 'That's probably his brother,' she said. 'The family lived in Taipei for a few years, and Sherlock once told me that Taiwanese Mandarin has become a code of sorts for them.'

'Shut up,' I said and she laughed.

'If I remember correctly, Mycroft suggested using Klingon but Sherlock couldn't be arsed to learn. Mycroft refused to speak to him for weeks after that.'

'Klingon,' I repeated, stunned. 'Mycroft speaks Klingon.'

'And Navajo.'

'What?'

'You think Sherlock's unusual? Wait until you get to know Mycroft.'

'But I've already met him. We had dinner together.'

'What did you think of him?'

'I thought he was an all right bloke.'

'Seriously? I must admit I find him a little creepy, with the way he measures you with his lizard eyes. Anyway, your friend's murder. I've been through the case file, and I understand Halabi was an investment genius with a special knack for identifying possible risks, and he worked in one of the top investment banks. Welcome back, Sherlock,' she said, as he emerged from the kitchen. 'How is your brother?'

'Mycroft is doing just fine, and he sends his love and hugs,' Sherlock replied and lowered himself into his armchair. 'There was something I needed to ask him.'

'What does Mycroft have to do with all of this?' I asked, not understanding.

'Mycroft knows things.'

'I see. And you know people who do stuff. Is that like Holmes, Inc.?'

'We do occasionally touch base, yes. You were saying, Lestrade?'

'I was about to say that the super is a member of a hiking group.'

'And who else might be in that hiking group?'

'I wouldn't know any names, but I understand it's a very select group of no more than 10 people, you know, top managers, Crown Prosecutors, judges, politicians...' She made a vague gesture. 'A tightly knit boys' club.'

'Would the CIO of an international investment bank be eligible for a membership of said boys' club?'

'I wouldn't know,' she shrugged. 'I'm merely...brainstorming.'

'It would be interesting to know whether the super had a lunch or dinner scheduled with anyone from that hiking group.'

'Yes, I believe that would be helpful,' Lestrade agreed. 'Listen, why don't you drop by tomorrow, and we talk about it at the station? Only, remember to not drop by between half-eleven and half-twelve. We have a fire drill scheduled during that time, and I will not be able to speak with you then. I don't know when exactly the drill starts, probably around a quarter to eleven.'

She crossed her legs. 'Good thing we have such thorough safety supervisors who make sure the offices are really empty. Oh, and I must remember to lock my computer. Just imagine if someone were to come by and hack into the network.'

'Imagine that,' Sherlock said, sounding bored. 'Are there any more king prawns left, or has John eaten them all?'

'No, Sherlock, I haven't,' I said and pushed the requested bowl his way. 'Eat, my boy. You'll need your strength for what's to come.'

'And what's that?' Lestrade asked interestedly.

The tips of Sherlock's ears grew pink, and he pretended to be too busy chewing.

'John?'

'I'm not at liberty to say,' I replied, grinning, and her mouth twitched.

When she finally left, we were on the best of terms, she and I. Gwen Lestrade was a down-to-earth person with a good sense of humour. She seemed genuinely fond of Sherlock, who did his best to appear the brat she teased him to be, but it was obvious he was fond of her too. I wondered what history lay between them, and I determined to meet up with her at a pub some day soon.

She had to have met him during the time he had described as *not so stable*; and, although I had a vague idea of what that might have entailed, I preferred to speak to her about it, rather than Mycroft.

'Don't break him, John,' she said with a mischievous twinkle. 'I still need him.' And, to Sherlock, 'Don't make him break you, Sherlock. I would hate to arrest a good man.'

'I won't,' I promised; and 'He won't,' said Sherlock, at the same time.

She looked from him to me and nodded, as if she'd seen something she approved of.

'See you around, boys.'

The front door slammed shut behind her, and Sherlock turned to me with an expectant look on his face.

'What is to come that you were not at liberty to say?'

'I'll show you,' I said and locked the door.

CHAPTER TWENTY-EIGHT

ABOUT A WEEK LATER, WE STOOD GROUPED AROUND SHERLOCK'S LAPTOP and stared at the screen in various states of disbelief. *We* included Djamal, Lina, Maik, and myself.

'He did what?' Lina asked, looking as stunned as I felt.

'When Karim linked his calculations, he noticed a faulty reference in his model. He cross-checked his links and found the IT infrastructure had changed; something that had been announced but the date of the actual move of the drives to the new server must have slipped his attention.'

'So the back-up data he needed wasn't on drive A but on drive B?' I asked, feeling like a computer Neanderthal.

'Exactly so. Only, the drive where he thought he had saved his data now contains sensitive material only the executive managers are supposed to have access to.'

'And I take it access rights had not been adjusted yet?' Maik raised his eyebrows, the lawyer in him already outlining a potential case.

'Exactly so,' Sherlock said again. 'What he found was not the groundwork for his deal, the transaction he had prepared for his Dubai business partners, but rather something of a far more interesting scale.'

'*Durnin McGhee*,' Lina read. 'Who is that?'

'They're distributors in the arms industry,' Maik said. 'Their Milan-based CFO is no stranger to my firm. And before anybody asks, the Milan subsidiary itself is exemplary where cooperation with authorities and such is concerned. It's individuals throughout the organisation who are rumoured to have their fingers where they do not belong.'

'Meaning?'

'Illegal weapons deals,' Sherlock said. 'Shipping things that go boom to people not supposed to have things that go boom.'

'Please tell me this is a sick joke.' Djamal had gone very pale. 'Are you implying that this... this stinking bank of his is supporting terrorist groups?'

'If it's fundamentalists you're thinking about,' Sherlock pulled up a name list, 'the answer is no. Think businesspeople, preparing the deal of a lifetime.'

'No way.' Djamal clenched his fists, obviously trying his best to keep calm.

'I wish it were otherwise,' Sherlock gently said. 'It would probably have all gone unnoticed if Karim hadn't reported his findings to the CIO. He thought it his duty to notify the board that sensitive material was pretty much out in the open. Fortunately for us, he downloaded everything he'd worked on without being aware he'd copied the entire file structure along with his actual work. Or maybe he was. I'm afraid that piece of the puzzle will never be found.'

'Where does the marketing bloke come in? Karim said he was all over him.'

'He and the CIO both got their degrees at Cambridge. Their wives are best friends, and their sons play football on the same team. I've not been able to find anything in the files I've seen, but I think it's a good place to start.'

'What do you intend to do with all of this?'

'That's why I asked you all here. It is not my decision what to do with a time bomb of that dimension. I can give you a full back-up of Karim's documents plus a copy of what's on the company's drive.'

'How did you come into possession of all of these documents?' Maik asked. 'Surely the drive's been extra firewalled and password protected by now?'

'Oh, never mind that,' Sherlock said dismissively. 'I've had a precision scalpel cut through the layers and lay everything open. Nothing's been removed from its original spot because something tells me we may still need everything in its home nest.'

'Maik.' Lina turned to her husband and spoke to him in rapid Arabic. Maik cocked his head and listened, his eyes darting from his wife to Djamal and back. If you squinted just so, you could see the proverbial dollar signs dance around his head.

Djamal uttered only one sentence but his voice shook with suppressed emotions, causing Lina to throw her arms around him and embrace him fiercely. Maik frowned but didn't say anything while Lina crooned at Djamal like one would at a heartbroken little boy.

'He wants to see the dogs hanged by their genitals,' Sherlock told me in a low voice. 'She wants to have their genitals sliced and bathed in saltwater, and then hang them from a rusty hook.'

Lina's eyes widened in shock, and Maik suffered a sudden coughing fit.

'Sorry,' Sherlock said. 'I tend to pick languages up fairly quickly.'

'I want to see these criminals rot.' Lina confirmed. 'Maik, do you think there's enough evidence to build a case?'

'Oh, I should think so. It would help having the documents delivered to my firm via a trustworthy source. Not that you are not trustworthy,' he added with an apologetic look. 'But deliveries with a more official character tend to be processed a bit quicker than those coming from private individuals.'

'The sender I intend to use guarantees hand-delivery to your desk or to anybody else's you think is best suited to handle this matter,' Sherlock said, a little haughtily.

'That would be me,' Maik replied in the same fashion.

'Then we understand each other.'

'I believe we do.'

Sherlock said something in Arabic that made Maik laugh and offer his hand. 'I would be honoured,' he said. 'I'm looking forward to playing with a worthy opponent.'

'What about this insurance that you told me about?' I asked. 'Wasn't there something about a life insurance policy the bank can cash in, bank-owned something?'

'The bank-owned life insurance? Yes, I found email correspondence in Karim's private mail folder. The premium was five million, which I believe is above average.'

Maik whistled. 'Not bad. Most are in the amount of one, maybe two million. That depends on the employee's status and benefits expected to be paid, a general risk assessment, and so forth.'

'Is it worth killing a man for? I mean, an investment bank certainly juggles sums much higher than that, right?'

Try as I might, I couldn't wrap my brain around it. It's one thing to watch a TV crime show, but quite another when your friend gets killed.

'People get killed for a lot less than that, John,' Sherlock said and closed his laptop. 'Greed is an ugly creature.'

He turned to Maik. 'Expect an express delivery by the end of this week. And think about who may want to sink their teeth into such a lovely piece of meat. Preferably someone who can go on very little sleep for a very long time.'

'I've got my team pulled together already. This is going to be fun.' His wife's eyes shot daggers at him, and he apologised for his inappropriate outburst. 'It is an interesting case, *habibti*. Your brother would have agreed.'

'He would have,' Djamal said. 'He loved riddles. The harder the shell, the more fun to crack.'

She sighed. 'I guess you're right. Well then, Sherlock, get your findings into the right hands to have them delivered to Maik's desk in style. And please send me your invoice.'

'Will do. Thank you for placing your trust in me.'

'You've earned it. It is I who has to thank you, and I do; from the bottom of my heart and on behalf of my family. Thank you.'

'I'm sorry I didn't have the chance to get to know Karim better,' Sherlock said. 'He was John's good friend and a brilliant analyst. The stuff he's worked on? Outstanding. I will do what I can to get my contact to drop a few words here and there. It just may speed things up a bit.'

'May I ask who your contact is?' Maik asked.

'You may, but I won't tell you,' Sherlock replied, smiling, and held out his hand. 'Don't forget to send me your details. I am much looking forward to beating you at chess.'

'And I look forward to letting you try.'

The Nairs left, and Djamal followed them after politely declining our invitation to join us for dinner. It was as I had feared; it was Karim's death that had briefly brought us together, but now that the case had been solved, we'd go our separate ways. I was sorry about that, but I knew that to pretend it was otherwise would have been foolish.

And so I watched him leave, the man my friend had loved and who had made him happy. I swallowed and blinked, my throat suddenly tight.

'You know, I hate to say it, but it actually wasn't Gregson's fault,' Sherlock remarked as he came to stand next to me by the window.

'What wasn't?'

'The snail's pace at which the investigation was going, or rather not going. He didn't even get a chance for his meagre efforts to go anywhere. He was stonewalled from way up high. Small wonder he was being such a miserable shit.' He gave me a searching look. 'Are you all right, John? We're still going out to eat, yes? I feel like I haven't eaten in weeks.'

I laughed, if a little shakily. 'Let's go then. I will not have you starve yourself.'

CHAPTER TWENTY-NINE

IT WAS RAINING THE DAY I WENT TO VISIT KARIM'S GRAVE. I HADN'T BEEN there since the funeral and hoped I'd find it again. I did, and, when I approached I saw a lonely figure standing there, palms pointing upwards in the traditional gesture of prayer. It was Djamal.

I waited at a respectful distance, and only when he lowered his hands, signalling his prayer was finished, did I walk up to him. His dark curls were plastered against his head, and he looked as if he was soaked to the bone.

'Hello John,' he greeted me. 'I've come to say goodbye.'

'What do you mean?' I asked, alarmed.

His smile was sad. 'Don't worry, I will not do anything fatal. I'm going to Canada on Friday.'

'Holidays?'

'No. I have accepted an offer from McGill University. They've offered me the post of senior lecturer at their linguistics faculty. I'll be teaching anthropological linguistics, focussing on classical and contemporary literature, you know, Arabic, Arab American, Arab Canadian, and so forth.'

'Wow, I'm impressed,' I said. 'Congratulations.'

'They asked me earlier this year but I declined.'

'Because of Karim?'

He nodded. 'I love teaching, and I'm especially interested in this particular field. Arabic literature and how it has changed, it's always been a hobby-horse of mine. But I had just met Karim, and I knew he was the one, you see. Sometimes you just know.'

'I know what you mean.'

'Yes, I know you do. You and Sherlock. Karim was so happy for you.' His voice threatened to break, and he cleared his throat. 'Anyway, they contacted me again two weeks ago because the person they had given the position to after I declined…well, it wasn't a good fit. I signed the contract last week and am flying over to discuss the curriculum, and some organisational stuff.'

'That sounds very good.'

'It is good, and I'm grateful. You don't often get a second chance.'

'No, you don't. Again, congratulations, Djamal. I'm sure you'll do fine.'

'I think I will. Eventually.'

He looked at the gravestone, then to the ground. He was standing in a puddle, and he stepped aside, as if he'd only just realised.

'I have to go now, John. I'm glad we got to meet. You're a good man, and it makes me thankful to know that Karim had such a good friend.'

'Likewise. I wish you all the best.'

He pulled me into a hug, catching me unawares and knocking my umbrella out of my hand, but I returned his hug and held on to him as tightly as he held on to me, knowing the moment he left, another tie to Karim would be severed. He must have felt it, too, but we did step away from each other eventually.

'Goodbye, John,' he said.

'Goodbye, Djamal. Be safe.'

He nodded, threw one last glance at the grave of the man he had loved, and turned to go.

I picked up my umbrella and followed him with my eyes until he turned around a corner and was gone. Then I turned to look at Karim's name on the simple tombstone.

'You know I don't know many prayers, let alone Muslim ones,' I said. 'And I'm not very good at this. But I wanted you to know that we found your back-up files, and Sherlock has managed to crack your encryption.

'Man, you dug up some serious shit. Your CIO and his marketing buddy are being taken apart by your brother-in-law as we speak. Maik is trying to hide it from Lina, but he's having such a good time ripping the wankers a second one. I hope the superintendent goes down with them, but Sherlock says he'll probably be pensioned off.

'Speaking of Sherlock, he would have loved to get to know you better. I have a feeling you two would have got along splendidly.'

I knelt down, carefully.

'I brought you something.' I reached into my pocket. 'I'm not sure if I'm supposed to do that because it's all so tidy here but what the hell.'

I placed the small white-and-blue droid figurine on the flat stone that covered Karim's grave. 'Your little friend here has provided us with everything we needed.'

I fell silent. I didn't know what else to say, and so I stood before Karim's grave for some more time. I don't remember whether I was saying a prayer for him, or whether I was losing myself in memories of some of the things we had done. But I do remember that when I finally turned to leave, the memory that I took with me was how he had hugged me and how he had waved at me with that bright smile of his.

It was a good memory to store away.

SHERLOCK WAS STANDING BY the cemetery gates, having a smoke and waiting for me. He stubbed the cigarette out when he saw me coming.

'Did you do what you came to do?' he asked.

'I did, yes. Djamal was there, too.'

'I know. I saw him on his way out. Told me he's going to teach at McGill. Good for him.'

He looked up to the sky and closed his ridiculous polka-dot umbrella. 'Look, it's almost stopped raining. Let's not take the bus. Let's walk home. It's not so bad anymore, is it?'

I reached for his hand, and he let me, even twined our fingers together.

'Let's go home, John,' he said again and squeezed my hand. I squeezed back, and he smiled.

'Yes, let's go home.'

Go home. With Sherlock.

No, it wasn't so bad anymore, all things considered.

THE END

ACKNOWLEDGEMENTS

I guess a few words of acknowledgement are in order, for there are those without whom this project would never have seen the light of day.

First and foremost, my most humble thanks to Atlin Merrick of Improbable Press who not only read but liked my fanfics well enough to approach me on a professional level, and to first encourage me to write a short story for their *A Murmuring of Bees* anthology, and then to scare the living daylights out of me by suggesting I should try my hand at a real story. Thank you, Atlin, thank you and thank you!

Then, there's Liza, Sandra, Simone, Bettina, and Dominique who listened to my endless ramblings and still encouraged me to keep writing. Claudia, for reading, feedback, and thumbs up. Dainelle, for challenging me to become a better writer. Peter, for a man's point of view. And last, but not least, my fantastic and very patient beta reader Maria who waded through all of my drafts and who kindly but mercilessly pointed out nonsense and errors, and an embarrassing number of typos. I'd be lost without my beta.

Thank you so very much, all of you!

Tessa Barding

Also from Improbable Press

AN IMPRINT OF CLAN DESTINE PRESS AUSTRALIA

www.improbablepress.co.uk

A QUESTION OF TIME
BY JAMIE ASHBIRD

Sherlock Holmes
whether he's a grimy student in 1980, a consulting detective in 47BCE, or a smitten neighbour in 1969, will always find his…

John Watson
whether he is a military doctor in 1917, an angry Saxon with an axe in 1086, or a priest in 1603.

A Question of Time is an illustrated journey through the ages told by our heroes, by their friends, and by a scorched manuscript.

A DREAM TO BUILD A KISS ON
BY NARRELLE M HARRIS

John Watson, invalided army doctor and sometime artist, and Sherlock Holmes, consulting detective, become flatmates and friends in contemporary London.

Love grows too, despite past betrayals and present dangers – for where you have Holmes and Watson, there too are Moriarty and Moran.

A Dream to Build a Kiss On explores love and family, trust and betrayal, brothers and brothers-in-arms, forgiveness and revenge, in an ongoing tale told 221 words at a time.

A Study in Velvet and Leather
by K. Caine

Sharing a flat with Sherlock Holmes should not have posed a problem for John Watson – after all, Watson is gay, Holmes is a woman, and the arrangement is financially convenient.

But when Holmes takes on a complex case involving Irene Adler and a scandalous photograph, she turns to Watson for assistance.

The case leads them everywhere from the opera to a secret Victorian BDSM club, and Watson soon finds himself questioning his partnership with Holmes, his sexuality, and his understanding of himself.

A Murmuring of Bees
edited by Atlin Merrick

Sherlock Holmes: mysteries, John Watson, and bees.

Here bees are front and centre in tales of secret diaries, rare nectars, and the private language of lovers, where John Watson and Sherlock Holmes are helping one another, romancing one another, *loving* one another.

Contributors: Amy L Webb, Anarion, Atlin Merrick, Brittany Russ, Darcy Lindbergh, Elinor Gray, Hallie Deighton, Jamie Ashbird, Janet A-Nunn, Kerry Greenwood, Kim Le Patourel, Kimber Camacho, Lucy Jarsdell, Meredith Spies, Morgan Black, Narrelle M Harris, Poppy Alexander, Stacey Albright, Tessa Barding, Verena, Verity Burns.

To encourage a world where such love is seen as the precious thing it is, profits from *A Murmuring of Bees* are donated to the It Gets Better Project.

THE ADVENTURE OF THE COLONIAL BOY
BY NARRELLE M HARRIS

It's 1893, and Dr John Watson, still mourning his friend after his death at the Reichenbach Falls, is now triply bereaved by his wife Mary's death in childbirth. Then a telegram from Australia interrupts his grief: *Come at once if convenient.*

Desperate to believe Holmes may still be alive, Watson takes an unexpectedly dangerous voyage to the Australian colony of Victoria.

And soon Holmes and Watson are racing through bohemian Melbourne, tackling a series of murders linked to a red leech and a remnant of Moriarty's gang. But things are not as they were.

Can Sherlock Holmes and Dr Watson solve a crime, save a life, rediscover trust…and admit to love?

SHERLOCK HOLMES AND JOHN WATSON: THE NIGHT THEY MET
BY ATLIN MERRICK

Some things belong together, the one with the other, natural pairs.

Sherlock Holmes and John Watson.

Whether it's in an empty house during the Blitz, a West London strip club in the 70s, or deep in the heart of a Hong Kong computer lab, the meeting of these two legendary men is inevitable.

Spanning 128 years, here are 19 stories of that destiny: of how, no matter where they are or when, a detective meets a doctor; of how they change each other in heart and mind; of how they fall in love.